Helical Symmetry

by Janina Arndt

Paperback ISBN 978-1-80424-772-3
ePub ISBN 978-1-80424-773-0
PDF ISBN 978-1-80424-774-7

Published by Orange Pip Books
335 Princess Park Manor, Royal Drive,
London, N11 3GX
www.orangepipbooks.com

Cover by Awan

Content

Prologue

221B Baker Street didn't exist in Victorian times. When the first stories about Sherlock Holmes were published, Baker Street didn't reach those numbers. Nowadays, of course, 221B is very much real and tangible. Yet, every time I wander close by, I'm scared to return to it; in case they have turned it into a museum.

I am aware that by telling our story, I am fulfilling the brief that the Victorian stories gave me. Dr Watson, the biographer of Sherlock Holmes. When we discovered the stories, I writhed at the thought. Now, I know that I am the only person able to tell the truth about him, and it is my duty to do so.

We were told, after everything was over, that it was all fake. His passport, his DNA, his fingerprints – the police and the council records returned nobody in existence. They couldn't even find his name, except in the stories.

Will you, dear reader, believe me now, whatever age you live in?

* * *

John can't tell the story alone. Not only is it the hardest thing he has ever done, but he wasn't there for all of it.

I was.

At first, I was the perfect case: a client, found with no memory, who had escaped from the criminal organisation known as The Red Circle. All John wanted to do was to prove me innocent, to love me again like he did when we first met, before everything, at university. And all Sherlock wanted was to solve my case, but he couldn't do it before the mystery of their lives appeared. It wasn't me. It was a story in *The Strand Magazine* about Sherlock Holmes and John Watson, that was written, set and printed 135 years before our time.

After that, all we wanted was to prove Sherlock Holmes and John Watson were real, not just words on a page.

It became harder when the stories started happening around us, with our hands tied, anchored to their course.

Slowly, not just the plot but the setting changed around us too. Victorian London drew in on us. There was the fog, but no machine. The gas lights, but no trace of their age. At the time, I thought I was the only one who wasn't in the stories – there is no character named Lily Scarlett Vendalle.

Now I know I can only save them if I enter the stories with them.

* * *

Scarlett was never her name. We should have known when she first told us that she was having visions of Anne Boleyn whenever she tried to remember her past life. We didn't know what it meant until it was too late. Not even Sherlock could figure it out.

Moriarty was always there, of course. When Scarlett was kidnapped just when we were growing close to solving her case, we realised how far away from reality we had been pulled trying to find out where our stories came from. When she began killing people from her past, we found ourselves in a story that was never in the books. We didn't need to prove we were real; we needed to find her.

* * *

It was hard to admit that I loved Sherlock as much as I loved John. Love was hard to admit. I had loved and lost in my past life. I couldn't let it happen again.

I'm sorry I lied to you, John. I will set this right. Trust me in this life.

Part 7: Mr Ashdown

Chapter 1

The doorbell rang through 221B Baker Street and echoed through our skulls. Neither of us moved.

There was a second ring. From behind folded hands, sitting in his classic pose on his favourite chair, Sherlock Holmes mumbled the word, 'Client.'

Still, we didn't move.

It had been three days since Scarlett had been kidnapped, and one since we had attended a crime scene with a suspect I couldn't convince myself wasn't her. Not everybody who escapes the life of a criminal organisation like The Red Circle really makes it out. Whether they had left her a choice to work for them or not, I didn't even know.

I also didn't know if I had saved the man she had shot; the police wouldn't tell us.

Sherlock still was unaware about my glimpse of her red hair, partly because I didn't want to believe what I had seen, and partly because I knew he wouldn't believe me either.

The doorbell rang through the house and our heads a third time, like a shout on a hungover morning. This time, Sherlock uncrossed and crossed his legs again in with his other leg on top this time.

Had it not been for Mrs Hudson forcefully knocking on our door, we would have, for the first time, ignored a client even before he entered. Sherlock often tried to assess and reject them based on his deductions about the person's arrival and auditory impressions when walking up the stairs, but so far, I had always convinced him to give everyone a chance.

Not so today.

Neither of us cared what this case was. We needed to find Scarlett. The likelihood of a missing person returning alive already falls drastically after the first 48 hours, and gets miniscule as the days go on. We knew we couldn't waste any time.

There was also the issue of our research or advances being blocked by the constant Victorianisation of our surroundings. Sherlock had got used to wearing his Inverness cape and dusty hats now. Perhaps we had even grown accustomed to getting into hansom carriages instead of black cabs here and there – the fog grew ever bigger. But the ongoing changes on the map of London, streets disappearing entirely or running a completely different route, names disappearing from the internet and others popping up that we could find in old books only made it very difficult to trace any leads.

I wasn't sure whether he had just been frustrated into a paralysis or given up on reality based on the fact that his deductions were leading us nowhere, but today, Sherlock hadn't moved from his armchair at all, and I was frankly at a loss on all fronts.

Mrs Hudson barged in, no longer content with being ignored.

'Really, it's not like you not to answer the door, I thought you might be dead!' Then, in a more pleasant manner, she turned to the tall man waiting uncomfortably in the narrow doorframe. 'Please, come in, Mr So. Mr Holmes will see you now.'

To our surprise, the man was wearing a dark grey, perfectly normal 21st century suit and tie. When Mrs Hudson banged the door behind her, I realised we still hadn't moved.

'Please do take a seat, Mr... So, was it?' I said, quickly pulling up a heavy wooden dining chair I could have clubbed Prince Albert to death with.

The man nodded with a smile and gratefully sat down. 'My name is Benjamin So, of So & Son Solicitors. I believe you may already know why I'm here.'

'What makes you think that?' Sherlock asked gruffly.

'We're not really seeing clients at the moment,' I excused my business partner. 'My name is...'

'Dr Watson, of course.' Mr So enthusiastically took my hand which I had almost pulled back at being recognised. He smiled again. 'I know, people often mistake you for one another, and then you have to explain and so on, it's very funny. Breaks the ice.'

I squinted at the man. 'How do you know all that?'

He laughed. 'I thought that's what I was supposed to say! It's my role to be surprised, isn't it? Now, Mr Holmes, tell me why I'm here. I can't wait to hear one of your brilliant deductions.'

Sherlock crossed his legs the other way again. 'Sorry, not interested.'

'In me or my case?'

'Either. As my partner Dr Watson here explained, we're not taking on any cases at the moment. Goodbye.'

I rolled my eyes. 'Don't be so rude, Sherlock. You've not made a single deduction, I can see it. And you, Mr So, had better tell us how you know so much about our conversation with clients. I presume we've helped someone you know?'

Mr So shook his head. 'Oh no, I thought it was rather obvious. I've read about you in *The Strand Magazine*! Really, I expected you to deduce as much, Mr Holmes.'

Here Sherlock sat up and tucked his hands under his chin. 'Please repeat what you just said.'

'I'm a big fan! Mr Holmes, please, you have to take on my case. The police won't help me, because he's only been missing for a few hours and I've always wanted to be one of your clients. Name the price and I will pay it.'

'You came here to consult us,' I said slowly, 'because you read stories about us?'

Benjamin So nodded vigorously.

'And what in those *stories* made you think we were real?' asked Sherlock, one eyebrow raised.

The man gestured towards him with both hands. 'But you are!'

'Give us a chance to find out before you jump to conclusions,' Sherlock mumbled.

Mr So ignored Sherlock's sinister comment. 'Please, Mr Holmes, you have to help me. You always do. Can you imagine a story where you just turn down a desperate man and do nothing?'

'That would be novel in the format, I suppose.' Sherlock threw a dark look at the skull on his mantlepiece.

'Dr Watson, please. A young man's life is at stake. There was a circle of blood on his desk this morning!'

I gasped. This was a sign often left by The Red Circle. Could this lead us to them and, through them, to Scarlett? Or, worse, was this case directly linked to Scarlett's disappearance?

Before I could convince Sherlock to take the case, he uncrossed his legs and said simply:

'If you wouldn't mind telling us everything you know about your legal administrator's disappearance. I'm a detective, not a psychic.' Sherlock put on a fake smile.

'This is what I love about you, Mr Holmes. How did you know it was my legal administrator?'

'You're carrying his business card in your jacket pocket. I can see the ending of his job title sticking out. Considering there aren't many types of roles in a soliciting firm, I fear this may have been a rather simple conclusion to jump to.'

'That's more like it!' cried our client. 'Now, where should I start? His name is Vincent Spaulding. He's always been a reliable employee – well, at least since he started working for me six months ago. You see, I did take a chance on him when he came to me seeking employment after he had served two years in prison for an armed robbery he fervently claimed he didn't commit. I believed him.

'Recently, he seemed to get restless and impatient with colleagues and clients alike. I didn't know what to make of it at first, but now I see that he must have felt like he was being followed. Now, I'm not so sure if his gang hasn't come for him. Either way, I assure you that he's really a good man and he wouldn't hurt anyone. Hence, why I believe he's in grave danger.'

'Was the circle of blood large enough to fit a head into the diameter of it?' I asked, remembering the last Red Circle victim we had found.

Mr So shook his head.

'If they had wanted to leave the body on the circle, they would have,' Sherlock interrupted. 'I'm afraid this does leave us the conclusion that this was a warning, but Mr Spaulding has not attempted to leave The Red Circle.'

'A criminal network we have encountered before,' I explained to our client.

'Do you have more data on your administrator, such as where he lives, how he commutes to work, anything that could lead us to where they might have intercepted him?'

'My business is on Fleet Street,' Mr So replied, 'and he lives at Saxe-Coburg Square.'

Sherlock and I exchanged glances. I could see he was taking this personally. He had apprehended a bank robbery a few years ago at Saxe-Coburg Square where he had anticipated the robbers to tunnel through from a nearby bank. The robbers had called themselves the red-headed league, due to their clown masks. As this story had already happened, it was hardly repeating itself now, I thought, but I was uneasy at the connection between The Red Circle and our previous cases.

'Would you mind if we made our way to Saxe-Coburg Square, Mr So? Please do feel free to wait here, it will be safer.'

'By no means, I'm coming with you!'

Sherlock rolled his eyes but didn't object.

To our surprise, Mr So had a black cab waiting for us outside. Sherlock and I both relished the purr of the engine.

Thick, industrial smoke hung in the air when we got off at our destination. It was nearly dark; one of the streetlights flickered in a way that made me unsure of its century of origin.

Among the brick houses, I recognised the City and Suburban Bank from our previous case, as well as the Vegetarian Restaurant and McFarlane's... carriage building depot? This was new to me, as was the pawnbroker shop.

Mr So walked over to house number 7 without even looking around and rang the doorbell. I was very close to asking him if he could see the Victorian buildings in the smog, but a warning look from Sherlock held me back.

'See, no answer at his door.' Mr So stepped back from the threshold. 'He isn't answering his phone either. I can't reach him at all.'

'I think we'd best enter to check on him,' Sherlock said, striding past his client and opening the door.

'How did you know it was unlocked!?' cried Mr So, rubbing his hands in anticipation of a deduction.

'Lucky guess,' Sherlock retorted gloomily as he followed his own story upstairs. 'No sign of a forced entry, though there are marks of a struggle on the wallpaper, which suggests Mr Spaulding knew his assailant and let them in. If I remember correctly, the door with the tunnel to the bank was next door?'

I nodded.

Inside the house, the door to the only room on the first floor stood open.

As he entered, Sherlock motioned me to stay with Mr So, but selfishly, almost hoping and not hoping at the same time that this was somehow connected to Scarlett, I simply followed, shutting the door in our client's face.

Mr Spaulding's body was curled up on the floor, stiff as if frozen in combat. His hands were at his throat. One didn't need to be Sherlock Holmes to figure out that he had been strangled with multiple strands of red hair which were still draped around his neck. The unfortunate man's own hair was matted with red paint.

The wall to our left had been knocked through crudely, as if someone was on the run and hadn't taken the lack of a door for a no.

When we heard Mr So try the door, Sherlock pushed him out immediately. 'I've seen everything I need here, please follow me.'

It was harder for me to do the same. I couldn't stop myself from touching the red strands of hair, trying to remember the feeling of Scarlett's. *Are we being led to her? Is she trying to give us clues?* My brain couldn't comprehend her being a killer again. All I wanted was to find her. Perhaps that was why I was so sure it was her.

When I returned to the Square, I could see in Mr So's face that Sherlock had broken the news.

'I just can't believe it! I only saw him yesterday.' Mr So clasped his mouth with one hand. 'What do you believe happened, Mr Holmes?'

Sherlock motioned to me to call Lestrade, before explaining what he had deduced.

'Unfortunately, Mr Spaulding was part of the gang that robbed the City and Suburban Bank. His real name was John Clay. It was John Watson and I who caught him, together with the police, who are on their way here now. Clay may have lied to you about the robbery, but it looks as though he had been trying to start an honest life in earnest after being released from prison. My suspicion is that someone in The Red Circle wanted to make use of the tunnel to the bank and contacted Clay to arrange matters. When he refused, he received the threat you found on his desk this morning. It seems as though he was too frightened not to let his assailant in, or perhaps he was too confident in thinking he could persuade them otherwise. When they insisted he follow through with their demands, he tried to block their way further into the house and was attacked, hence the scratches on the walls downstairs.

'As there are no marks on the stairs, the landing or the door on the first floor, I would wager he gave in and led them upstairs to the wall which adjoined the room above the tunnel in the neighbouring house, No. 8. Here it would seem that, despite giving away this information, he was nonetheless attacked from behind and strangled in cold blood.

'The assailant then knocked through the wall and disappeared down the tunnel. Considering there have been no reports of another robbery today, the culprit used the tunnel as an escape route from this crime, and that the unfortunate Mr Spaulding's murder was their only objective. The warning circle of blood was not for him but for everyone else investigating this crime not to mess with The Red Circle. They like to leave signatures.'

Mr So stared at the ground for a good while before he finally spoke, 'I suppose even you can't save everyone, Mr Holmes.'

Sherlock pursed his lips. 'I never claimed I could.'

As police sirens approached in the distance, Benjamin So looked back up at Sherlock Holmes and shook his hand. 'I thank you, nonetheless. If it weren't for this outcome, I would say this was one of the most exciting days of my life. Mr Holmes, you have no idea how happy I am to have met you, and to have seen your powers for real. The world is a better place with you in it.'

Sherlock was scratching his chin when Mr So left to give a statement at the Yard. Lestrade did not ask us to come along but wanted an informal statement instead. He could tell we weren't going to say anything officially. We hadn't said a word after the man had been shot at the pool.

'Come on, Sherlock,' the inspector said now. 'There's got to be something you can tell us. You clearly figured out what happened or else you wouldn't be here. At least give us an anonymous tip or something!'

The flickering street light threw shadows of doubt on Lestrade's pleading face.

Sherlock put on a false smile. 'Would you believe me if I said the killer was a six-foot-five wrestler in a tutu?'

'No.' Lestrade pulled a face.

'Then there's no need to write down anything I say.' The consulting detective patted the detective inspector on the shoulder and motioned for me to follow him into the grey fog.

Chapter 2

I don't remember much of the rest of the day. Sherlock found no one, and neither did the police.

She had escaped again, I was convinced.

I perceived everything through a gloomy fog, which perhaps I was wishing had clouded my view when I had seen those red strands of hair.

When we came home, Mrs Hudson tried to cheer us up without success. Our smiles were weak even when she produced Sherlock's old, modern coat out of the blue. I forgot where she had found it. When I asked her again later, she told me it wasn't Sherlock's but her late husband's coat. I also forgot how peculiar it was for them to have the same clothes.

In the evening, Sherlock sat down with me to talk about my shock. This was bizarre in itself, because it had never happened before, but I was too numb to think about it.

'It was her. I saw her, Sherlock, at the pool,' I finally managed.

'I know,' he said carefully. 'Whatever you think, John, whatever you saw, we can't be sure it was her. What exactly did you see?'

It took me a moment to answer. 'Her hair.'

Sherlock bit his lip. After a while, he said, 'John, we know this is connected to her, but still, I'm convinced it can't have been her. What you saw confirms that hypothesis: she would've pinned up her hair. And besides, I told you she could hardly be in a state to run around killing people who have been trained in the same business on top of it. No, I rather think this Eamonn Doyle is trying to distract us. But I've got all the Irregulars on the lookout and I

13

promise you that once we've got a proper lead – and that *will* turn up – we'll find her.'

'And what if it *was* her and you're just missing something?'

'It *wasn't* her,' he said through clenched teeth, then seemed to compose himself. 'John, don't jump to conclusions. If we find her and she tells you she was locked up the entire time, you can go and live with Mycroft if you don't believe her.'

I was rather taken aback by this sudden defence of the criminal woman I loved. Maybe I didn't want to allow myself to believe it wasn't her, because I wanted it so much it could hardly be true. Sherlock had a point, though. How many times had I seen him prove obvious evidence for one scenario to reveal a completely different truth? I had one more question though.

'What if she remembers everything now?'

The focus in Sherlock's eyes evaporated. Then the echo of a smile wavered across his firm lips.

'Then we catch him.'

We spent the next few days with Toby who was trying to hack the file of this ominous Eamonn Doyle. Sherlock also occupied himself with figuring out the most likely hiding place according to the latest faked data. Then we went to each location only to find Lestrade already there or on his way. Every place was somehow connected to our previous cases. Sherlock insisted on the fact that these spots were just very convenient for murders – empty houses, old warehouses, hidden cellars, public buildings closed at night.

The more places we saw, the more my mind started to see Scarlett in them. I started having nightmares. Scarlett breaking into our flat at night, apologising for what she had done, telling me the truth, which I forgot, only to kill me in the end. Another showed Scarlett in the street, getting shot by one of her victims. Then, Scarlett in my bed, lying to me, telling me she'd never been away. I started up every time I looked into her eyes. When I woke, I still saw them clearly before mine. Quiet horror of knowing these eyes didn't belong to her, but recognising her face all the same. It was as if I was seeing two different people. There was a crack in my memory of her features now.

* * *

Eamonn had been torturing and kissing me in turns. The difference tore me apart. When he kissed me, I remembered why I had loved him, and loved him to death.

It was so easy to give in to him. No restraint, no rules. It was like discovering a new continent, redefining the composition of the air, escaping fate. Back when I was younger, I hadn't realised that by escaping fate *with him*, he would become fatal to me.

And when he tortured me, I remembered I deserved all this. I remembered the faces of the people I had killed. Now that I could feel their pain, I could not help but feel that they could not have burnt the world and deserved it more than me.

What pained me the most, however, was to see Sherlock and John in my mind, despairing over my state. I could only ever be a terrible deception to them. In the end, I had to wish I'd never met them and dragged them into this trap.

I was bleeding out on the floor again. My hands were tied, my last bit of strength gone, and my body unable to move. I hadn't said a word to Eamonn. At least, I had not betrayed them; no pain had tempted me. If I was to die now, at least I knew there was nothing more I could have done. In the end. *Is this it?*

My eyelids closed, the sound echoing in my skull. I had deafened my ears with my own screams. My mind was buried in evidence of my guilt. I hoped delirium would come for me in my sleep.

Eamonn came to bid me goodnight. No, I was not certain he was really there, in the flesh... I had none left. But I felt...

Eamonn's cold hand on my
cheek, his
gaze piercing both our eyelids, before
stabbing my mind...

He kissed the mental wound...

his lips renewing life in
mine as he touched
them...

He kissed my cheek...

my jaw...   my bleeding ear...
my pain was
lost in awe of his   intimacy...
deconstruction of my suffering...

deadly remedy...

And yet... there was knowledge of the
toxicity in his lips...

but...

regret of their
fatal consequence in the tension
around their corners...

his lethal lips...

...bent upwards in his inevitable smile...

* * *

16

With every further hour, I stumbled nearer to the brink of insanity. And it didn't help that Sherlock didn't seem far away from it either. Our scavenger hunt had amounted to less than nothing. I couldn't get myself to care an ounce for the heap of dead members of that dubious brotherhood, The Red Circle, and Sherlock wasn't in the least tempted by working on that end any more than what concerned our search for Scarlett.

We were utterly and completely lost. In some moments, I suspected Sherlock was using drugs again – 'Just for the case,' he would probably say – but I didn't stop him. There was nothing I had the strength to do, nothing that still seemed to be in my power. Nothing at all.

It was not until the following day that Sherlock figured it out. It was raining heavily outside, and we were standing in yet another empty house, a corpse at our feet. I hadn't been at all sure whether Sherlock was in a fit state to go anywhere, but he had been as persistent as ever when Toby had texted him.

'We can find her. Never doubt that, Watson. Never that.'

I didn't even complain that he was calling me Watson.

Now, he was cowering down next to the dead man, lifeless features on both sides of his magnifying lens.

'Well?' I asked tentatively.

No answer. I cleared my throat. Still no answer.

'Sherlock?'

He kept on scanning the body, checking the man's pockets, his hair, his throat...

'Ha! I've got it, John!'

'*What is it!? Tell me, now!*'

'I *would* if you stopped shouting at me! Here. Do you see those marks?' There was a black hyphen with a dot on either side on the body part Sherlock was pointing my attention to.

'A tattoo, yes. What about it?'

17

'It's an R in Morse. Moriarty's code for the reinforcement unit.'

'Does that mean Moriarty's behind all this?'

'No, John, it doesn't. This tattoo is fresh, don't you see? It's our messenger trying to make it look like Moriarty again.' Sherlock pulled down the man's sock. 'See, the tattoo on the ankle is older, less shiny. Tattoos only shine for a few weeks. We have to get back to the other bodies we've been called to and see whether we've overlooked something.'

And in a flash, we were racing down the road in Lestrade's car to meet Mike at the morgue. He greeted us at the entrance, and, Sherlock having phoned him, he had prepared the bodies for us.

'Steven was the last to lock the doors yesterday, but this time no one got stolen,' Mike tried to joke.

I gave him a weak smile.

'Well, what are we looking for?' he asked.

'Tattoos,' Sherlock replied, as inscrutable as ever. 'Someone broke in late last night and tattooed these bodies.'

'Oh, right.' He just accepted that Sherlock didn't want to elaborate, and I was grateful for it.

Sherlock, meanwhile, had started dancing about with his lens, and soon found what he had expected. 'John, get something to write. This is an A. What would it be an A for?'

'An A?' Mike was now confused.

'In Morse,' I added trying to keep him from further questions.

'OK.' He fetched me a notepad and a pen.

'Ta.' I took them and wrote down an A immediately.

'E!' Sherlock shouted, rushing to the next body. 'Write down the R we just found as well.'

What was this supposed to be? A message on bodies? I stepped closer to see whether Sherlock hadn't gone nuts, but I could see the fresh tattoos as well. These seemed even shinier than the other one.

'K!' Sherlock yelled out. I tried to make something of the letters, but neither the word *rake* nor any other combination of the letters made sense to me.

'T!'

Well, that didn't help much more. *A trek? No... How would that be a clue?*

'Oh, God...' Sherlock was standing next to the sixth body, breathing heavily, dropping his lens.

'For God's sake, *talk*, Sherlock! What is it!?'

'Baker Street...'

'What!?'

But Sherlock just shoved me out of the room, running down the corridor, dragging me along. Without Lestrade's permission, he threw himself into the driver's seat of his car. 'Baker Street, now!' Rushing home, he started explaining away. 'A dash and three dots, the sixth body was marked with a "B". Someone was spelling out Baker Street. The bodies have been tattooed within the last 24 hours. This is a deliberate clue, but not by the killer. Someone else. Maybe the person who altered the files of her ex.'

Scarlett.

'Do you think we'll find her in Baker Street now?'

'If we do, there's not a moment to lose.'

He accelerated even more. The other cars quickly started to keep a safe distance from us. Sherlock's driving style was dangerous, but he seemed to have the vehicle under control.

In front of 221B, he pulled the hand brake, almost sending us flying. Then we ran up the stairs. Sherlock was faster, and nearly broke down the door to our living room.

'Don't! Go around that corner.'

Instinctively, he extended his arm to shield me from this view. His eyes were fixed upon what his shock made him unable to name.

'Sherlock, I'm not a child anymore!' I screamed, pushing him aside, but he held me back again, and looked me straight into the eye.

'*You don't want to see this.*'

I didn't take it seriously. He couldn't stop me as I rushed past him.

'Who cares what I want—'

There she was, lying on the floor, her thorax resting against the armchair, her body covered in cuts, blood soaking her clothes and the carpet. Three cards were randomly fitted into three cuts. The tips of her open, fiery hair touched the floor. She was pale as death.

I was paralysed.

My eyes riveted themselves to Sherlock in search of something to hold on to. He had immediately turned around and pressed his hands to his face as if to delete what had just burnt itself into his mind. His fingers were clawed deeply into his eye sockets. Then he sharply turned again.

Regaining the ability to move my limbs, I knelt down next to Scarlett, feeling her pulse. It was so weak that I could've been imagining it. With a quivering hand, I took out my keys and held them to her mouth to see whether they would mist over.

Nothing.

I couldn't breathe.

My eyes turned to Sherlock again. Motionlessly, he stood there, his eyes and nostrils wide open. Slowly, his face started to seal again as he moved towards us. His coat was what seemed to pull him down to his knees in the pool of blood.

Finally, I managed to force myself to look at Scarlett again. The keys were misting...

'Thank goodness!'

The next moment, my phone was at my ear. 'Watson here, we need an ambulance at 221B Baker Street quickly. A young woman, severe bleeding.' Then, I rose to get the aid kit.

When I had covered Scarlett's wounds with bandages as well as I could, I went back into the kitchen to fetch her a glass of water. For Sherlock, a preserving instinct inside me made me get a glass of brandy. I'd never seen him in such a state. He'd failed to solve the case. He almost seemed to feel guiltier than me. If Scarlett survived, it was only because whoever had placed her here had wanted her to. There was absolutely nothing we could do now but wait.

I knelt down next to her again. Her beautiful cold features seemed chiselled into marble. Fearful symmetry. I had to look away.

'Drink something,' I told Sherlock – to do *something* in my despair – but he wouldn't move. '*Please.*

He drank up the brandy and slowly rose to look out of the window, giving me some privacy.

My heart contracted as I touched Scarlett's icy cheek. Her waxen skin froze the blood in my veins.

The sound of crushing glass made me start. Sherlock let go of the fragments in his hands.

'What the *hell*, Sherlock, you are bleeding!'

'She's bleeding.'

With that, he left the room, but his voice rang in my head. None of this could be happening.

* * *

'It's a miracle she is alive. Most people would have been dead long ago. She must have a strong will to live.'

21

A blurry image of people without faces, dressed in white, forced itself into my brain.

Where am I?

What are you doing to me now?

Eamonn?

I couldn't distinguish between the wavering forms. My body felt as if someone had set it on fire. The heat soon deprived me of any clear thought until I passed out from the smoke of my own flames. Anne covered my consciousness with her shawl, only to reveal her neck to the executioner. Paralysis took hold of me when he lopped off her soul.

* * *

I'd spent all night by her bedside. Sherlock had waited outside the room, in case I needed him. When she woke up in the morning, I was so tired I thought I was dreaming.

'J-John,' she croaked with a broken smile, her clear grey eyes gazing into mine with an equal amount of guilt.

I almost burst into tears. Afraid that I would hurt her if I touched her, I could do nothing but stare at her.

With great effort, Scarlett managed to place her cut-up hand on top of mine. The edges of her wounds almost seemed to stab into my skin. Sherlock had spared me the deductions about her torture, but even I could draw my conclusions.

'John...' she tried again, struggling to articulate, 'Will you... promise me... one thing?'

I shook my head at her even having to ask. 'Anything.'

'Promise me... not to... blame... yourself... for this? And to stop... Sherlock... from blaming... himself? I I... know you... both do, but... I remembered... enough now... It's my own... fault, believe me... I don't... deserve to be... saved...'

She remembered.

My helpless attempts at clinging to her amnesic innocence failed. *She remembers... enough.? What memories are missing then.?* I didn't dare to ask, scared that she might go into shock again. When I had pulled myself together to look at her again, Scarlett was smiling, but she couldn't completely conceal how pained she was by my grief.

'You tell Sherlock everything, alright?'

She nodded gravely.

When I closed the door behind me, Sherlock immediately rose. 'How is she?'

'Very weak. She can speak though. Sherlock, she said she remembers enough not to deserve saving. I need you to find out what that means.'

'It means she's been tricked. Don't believe a word she says.'

I took a deep breath and sat down. I could only hope he was right.

Before Sherlock went in, he quickly added, 'John, she's been trying not to frighten you, but I'm sure she will tell me more.'

'How would you know?'

'John, she's been abducted and tortured but she's still alive. In such a state as we found her, she can hardly have overcome her kidnapper. Conclusion is that whoever did this to her is still out there. She might want to warn us.'

'If there's anything she can warn us about... Who knows what she saw?'

'She remembered things. It wouldn't be the first time someone used her memories as clues.'

'Just don't you give her a panic attack, or I'll punch your lights out.'

Ignoring me, Sherlock knocked at the door. 'May I come in?'

A quiet 'Yes' came from inside.

I closed my eyes.

* * *

It was a blessing to see Sherlock's face. His large, dark curls bobbed up and down unperturbed by his haggard face. I could see he'd been suffering as much as John, but he was better at putting on a front. While I couldn't deny my responsibility for John's suffering, Sherlock somehow managed to create the illusion that I was not responsible for his.

He quietly sat down in the chair next to my bed and took my bandaged hand. One of his was bandaged, too. In his crystalline grey eyes, I could see that he had stopped blaming himself for a moment.

'I'm glad you're awake,' he said gently, allowing politeness to give me some normality.

'Me too.'

His thumb soothingly stroked the back of my hand. A small, kind gesture. Suddenly, I was scared it was hurting him.

'What happened to your hand?'

'I failed...' His voice was glass. 'I'm sorry I didn't find you earlier.'

I placed the tip of my index finger on his lips. He briefly smiled.

'John said there was something you wanted to tell me.'

'No, you said there was something I wanted to tell you. I know John told you... and I know you figured out I want to warn you, but don't tell him for the moment.'

'I won't.'

'You know about... Eamonn, don't you?'

He nodded again.

'I don't know where I was. Some underground office, I think. It was so quiet... He kept me there, tortured me for information. He wanted me to confess what you knew about him. But I... I didn't. You have found out who he is by now, haven't you?'

'Yes.'

For a second, I could distinguish a split in his gaze. Everything seemed to play in his mind like a film. He opened and closed his mouth, then grimaced, probably having figured out the last few clues he had been missing.

'Well,' I quickly continued, 'Eammon didn't believe you didn't know about my past, of course, but I didn't care. He got nothing out of me. At first, I thought he was just scared you might get him arrested during some important job he had coming up or something. But one night, he thought I had passed out already and spoke to one of his accomplices.'

'What did he say?'

'I couldn't swear to the exact words, but he said that he knew I was lying, because you'd hacked into his file and the only way to stop you was to stick to the story. But he kept demanding the same things, whether you'd seen his file, knew his name, although he already knew. I think he wants me to lead you to him. You know I won't show you the way to your own death, don't you?'

Sherlock gave me a regretful smile. 'I know.'

'Please, keep John safe while I'm here. Don't go after Eamonn. I need you to promise me to wait until I'm well again. Well enough to make a plan at least. And take Lestrade with you.'

'We will.'

He rose, mindfully spreading his long fingers across my cheek, and bent down to kiss my forehead. I could feel all his

25

strength gathered up in his restraint. When he let go, he coated his smile in politeness to save me from harm. Then, swiftly, he left.

Chapter 3

Of course, Sherlock didn't tell me what she'd said. I felt very much like throwing him out of the window at first, but then he said she'd had him promise he wouldn't tell me and I almost jumped out the window myself.

'I told you she's trying to be kind to you, letting you recover from the shock. And it is the least we can do not to let her feel responsible. I need to find something out, one missing piece; once I have it, I'll tell you what she said.'

In the evening, Scarlett seemed noticeably improved. When Sherlock came back from his enquiries with his Irregulars, she asked him to sit down next to us.

'There's something neither of you are telling me. Suspense is not relaxing. Spit it out.'

Seeing that she could now get through several sentences without gasping for breath, I finally opened up:

'Scarlett, there's been a series of murders in London. All victims were members of The Red Circle and found in locations where Sherlock and I already solved a crime together. Sherlock says the killer is a woman, about 5'6".'

Scarlett lifted her eyebrows incredulously.

'No, we haven't told the police about that last detail,' Sherlock assured her.

'You don't think I could've murdered people sleepwalking?'

'No, we don't. Whoever did this wasn't sleepwalking. Besides, considering the state you are in, it is safe to say you've been physically incapable of committing the murders. However, we located the crime scenes by evaluating data from Eamonn

Doyle's file. Someone changed it whenever a new murder happened. Based on the clues in there, we found it simultaneously with the police, who, of course, were called when the bodies were discovered. So, yes, it is connected to you after all. We found the last body two days ago – shortly before you appeared in our flat – because someone had been so kind as to leave the clue "Baker St" tattooed on the victims. Now, we need to know everything you can remember about the past few days to the smallest detail. Your alibi may depend on it, despite my reasoning.'

She told us all about the place she'd been kept in, what she'd remembered about her past life, what exactly her victims had looked like, the surroundings, the weapons, the orders she'd had in her mind. But, understandably, she was unable to speak about the torture.

Everything sounded believable, and it seemed impossible for her to have been the killer. Yet, I kept remembering her fluttering fiery hair at the pool, and couldn't but recognise her step. My instinct kept nagging me with the notion that I had known the person running, and strangely, whatever she or Sherlock said couldn't erase that impression. She wasn't lying; I was sure of that. But she couldn't tell us everything, and Sherlock and I both knew there was more to it.

That night, I stayed with her to keep watch. I couldn't undo her kidnapping, but I was not letting it happen again.

The next morning, Sherlock showed Scarlett the picture of Eamonn Doyle we had found in his file. She didn't recognise it. Toby's hacking into the police database hadn't produced any matches either. Now we had to rely on her description of him. It was painful to watch her recall his features. Her eyes kept blinking, oscillating between light and darkness, fear igniting on her face.

'He had short, black hair or maybe just dark? I... didn't see very well. Dark eyes, beady, pale skin, small nose, full lips...' she stated, remembering in between. It was visible, even now, how she had loved this monster.

'How tall is he?' Sherlock asked.

'A bit taller than John, but shorter than you.'

I gave her a handkerchief. We didn't press any further at first, but when a while later she seemed a bit stronger, Sherlock told her the man who'd hit her with his car seemed to be identical with Eamonn Doyle.

'No!'

'Yes.'

'But how? That man was much taller. I'm absolutely sure. Unless I was dreaming all this, I'm positive those men weren't one and the same.'

We had no idea what to make of it.

It took several days until Scarlett had recovered enough to leave the hospital. Nonetheless, her strength was remarkable. Mike and Mrs Hudson kept visiting her, which considerably lifted her spirits. Especially our landlady's biscuits, which seemed to have a vitalising effect.

During these days, we followed Lestrade's investigation into the murders, but didn't take part ourselves. On the day we were finally allowed to take Scarlett home, however, the day I thought everything would be well again, our mystery came back at us. When we opened the door of 221B, Mrs Hudson was nearly crying and kept beckoning us to our rooms.

'They've got a warrant! Please, tell me what's going on.'

'What!?' I exclaimed, while Sherlock dryly remarked, '*They'll* have to tell us.'

We carefully walked into the living room, Sherlock leading the way, protectively extending his hands as if to shield us. The flat was in complete chaos. Our books were scattered all over the place, every drawer emptied onto the floor, the carpet ripped up at the edges. Nobody was to be seen, but we could hear that Scotland Yard had gathered in the kitchen.

What on Earth are they doing there?

Sherlock and I slowly scanned every corner for cues that might trigger Scarlett. She was still very vulnerable, but she had insisted on coming back home because she wouldn't have us sleep in chairs for another week.

We found Lestrade and several other people gathered in one corner by the kitchen door, staring at something we couldn't see. Occasional 'Ah's and 'Oh's came from the small crowd. On thinking twice, it occurred to me: were they looking at Scarlett's *file?*

Sherlock, of course, had understood immediately, and now addressed me very quietly. 'You stay with Scarlett; watch out she doesn't go into shock. Sit her down somewhere. She's exhausted already. I'll go talk to them.'

I nodded, taking Scarlett into the corner furthest away from the kitchen and replacing Sherlock's armchair for her. She looked at me with wide eyes.

'This is because of me, isn't it?'

I bit my lip and looked out of the window.

'Oh my God,' she gasped. 'You know *why* this is happening, don't you? John, talk to me! You look like you saw me murder someone!'

In her shock, her voice broke away from her head on the last syllable. I could've punched myself for giving this away. Her pain hit me like a truck.

'You do think I did it, don't you? That's why you've been asking all these questions!'

At first, I didn't know what to say, then: 'I... saw nothing. Just... Do you remember anything about a pool?'

'No, John. Not a thing! You have to believe me!' She clutched my arm. 'What about it?'

30

'We... I found a man there. He was almost dead. Someone had shot him in the stomach.' I took a deep breath. 'And when I tried to help him, I saw...'

My voice gave way. Her grip tightened. I tried again.

'Someone ran around the corner next to us. I could hardly see anything. The light was so bright, but I saw you— your hair fluttering through the air. I'm sorry, I shouldn't have told you at all. Sherlock keeps saying it couldn't have been you, and I know he's right. I know you're not lying. But I also know whoever this Doyle fellow is, he managed to trick us several times and I wouldn't be surprised if he tricked you.'

Scarlett winced at the thought. I knew I was being cruel to her, but now there was no way of undoing this again. Very quietly, she seemed to sink back into herself, thinking back at those horrible days she'd spent in that cellar.

After a while, she slowly shook her head. 'You have to believe Sherlock. It can't have been me. It *can't.* I would *never* do such a thing again! Not for anything in the world!.' She pulled me down by my upper arm until I was kneeling, eye-level with her. 'John, look at me. You have to believe me. I won't be able to live with myself if I've turned into such a monster again!' She clutched my collar. 'And even less so if you thought this of me, true or not.'

I kissed her. The only way I could think of to redeem her. It was presumptuous to think I could bestow redemption, but I wasn't in my right mind. She firmly wrapped her hand around my neck. I buried my hands in her hair to convince myself it was not the same as I had seen. For a second, I was convinced. The next moment, I regretted the thought.

'No! John doesn't know about it!' Sherlock's desperate shouting tore us apart.

A lot of ruffling was to be heard, and a thump, then silence. I could distinguish Sherlock's quick, fearful breath. A beat. Then we heard Lestrade's sad voice.

'On your head, Sherlock.'

A few shuffling feet. My blood froze with apprehension.

Next, Lestrade came into the living room. He looked plain sad, but I could see there was nothing he could do but his duty. 'I'm terribly sorry for being here, and I'm sure there will be a reasonable explanation for everything, but for now, I'm afraid I'll have to take you to the Yard.'

'What do you think you're doing? Scarlett's been tortured and now you want to arrest her for it!?' There was no way I would let that happen. Scarlett was clinging to me tightly.

'I'm sorry, believe me, I am. But the evidence leaves me no other choice.'

'What evidence? Look at her - she's evidence enough that she didn't do it!'

'Can you give her an alibi?'

'What?'

'You can't.' Lestrade unhappily cast down his eyes. 'We found her DNA at two of the crime scenes, and on the jacket of the man you saved. There's nothing I can do for her at the moment.'

Scarlett had started shaking violently, now staring at Lestrade in shock. She couldn't speak a word, nor did she let go of me. I held her tight, not moving an inch, but my heart had plummeted below ground. I felt guilty beyond measure for not believing her, and it almost felt like this had put Lestrade on her trail. He didn't try to urge us, but to justify himself a little, although he didn't seem entirely convinced of her guilt himself.

'She's... on record in Bolivia. Their authorities found the match. She had no criminal record in England before, but now that this happened, I have no choice.'

'Just a bit of DNA!? It could've been planted there!' I argued.

'It wasn't. We checked. Even Sherlock would say the same if he'd seen it. And I'm again sorry to say this, but there's something else. We found a file.'

Scarlett flinched but could only claw her fingers to the wreck those words had left of me. I was shattered. It was my fault. I had looked at her file during our investigations. I'd been too overwhelmed to hide them again properly, so I'd just tucked them among the magazines in a shelf. Had I only known...

After a silent while, Lestrade continued. 'Checked with the Bolivian authorities. The data corresponds with the crimes the police there suspected her to have committed. Sherlock insists you didn't know what's in there. Since I can't prove it very easily, I'm not going to try right now. But whatever way we look at it, John, she killed several people.'

'She lost her memory!'

'I know, I know. But it's not for me to decide what to convict her of. I have to do my job or more people might die.' Lestrade gulped at his own words, miserably looking away. Then he addressed Scarlett, 'If there's anything you can tell me that might alleviate your guilt, Scarlett, I'd be very grateful. If somebody made you do this, or anything else... Just tell me. Once you feel ready that is. Please, stay in this room now. My people are investigating one other thing at the moment. We need to wait for an expert. As long as you're here, you can take all the time you need. I suppose, you two might want a moment with Sherlock.'

Politely, Lestrade retreated into the kitchen and sent Sherlock over to us. The door banged shut.

'Why did you tell him I didn't know?' I asked Sherlock blankly.

'It's the least I could do. Should've burnt her files long ago...'

Another long silence.

Finally, Scarlett spoke up. 'Does this mean they're arresting you, too?'

Sherlock nodded, giving her an almost unnoticeable, sad smile. 'For holding back evidence, obstructing the police investigation, misleading the authorities... Could be worse.'

'Why didn't you just say you'd never seen the files either? They could've just been mine.'

'You've got enough to worry about. Besides, Lestrade was with us when we found the files. I tried to hide it from him at that moment, and there was no other way I could protect John, but saying they're mine.'

Sherlock wouldn't budge. I just wished I could've been arrested instead, because it was my fault, and also because I wanted to be with Scarlett, but my friend was right. He'd be arrested anyway sooner or later, and they would need someone who could help from the outside.

A few minutes later, Mrs Hudson showed upstairs a very serious looking man in a suit and tie, carrying a big brown leather case. When he had vanished into the kitchen to attend to Scotland Yard's needs, she came over to us with a fearful look.

'What's this man doing here? He said he was some sort of expert... Sherlock, please tell me this is not some kind of drugs bust again.'

'I wish it were. It's the guinea pigs' charms. B and M. You remember them, John?'

I nodded. When Scarlett had first been found unconscious and without her memory, they had found her guinea pigs hopping around in their travel cage next to her. It was obvious they had been planted there. The notorious criminal Moran had made sure that they were returned to Scarlett at 221B after we had lost them in a chase; Sherlock had suspected something about the little golden letter charms each of them was wearing on their collar.

'B and M. Benedict and Martin, wasn't it?'

Scarlett slowly nodded, too, but Sherlock contradicted:

'It's not that. It's not about their names at all. Actually, it's not B and M either, but M and B -Mary Boleyn. They belong to the necklaces of Anne Boleyn's sister. Hence, Scarlett's visions. The existence of Anne's A and B necklaces are historically proven. The B necklace even appears in her portraits. Her sister was very likely to have had one with her initials, too. I can't believe I didn't stumble onto that earlier. You probably got them on some black market, before you lost your memory.'

'So that's why they kept planting the guinea pigs on us,' I realised.

'Exactly. There were two trails that led the police here. Moran must have nudged them in the direction of the necklace charms once the murders started. Made sure we would be arrested in any case,' Sherlock concluded grimly.

Mrs Hudson gasped at his last remark. 'Are you trying to tell me they're here to arrest you all!?'

Sherlock gently put his arm around the old lady's shoulders. 'Not John. But Scarlett and I will have to go. I'm sorry.' He soothingly stroked her arm. 'You'll have to be very brave and help John get us out again. He'll know what to do.'

'*The hell* do I!' I blustered.

'I instructed my Irregulars to search all the crime scenes for evidence again. You need to find out where they kept Scarlett. That's the only way we can provide a solid alibi.'

'But what about the files?'

'Try and get Mike to identify them as counterfeit. I'll manage the rest.'

I wasn't actually sure that his plan would work, but I was grateful for something to cling onto. Then Sherlock mindfully turned his and Mrs Hudson's back on Scarlett and me, engaging her in some kind of absorbing conversation, which gave us some privacy.

'You'll take care of yourself, won't you,' Scarlett asked anxiously, running her hand through my hair.

'Yeah,' I whispered, my voice almost gone.

I think both of us wanted to speak, but couldn't find the courage. Scarlett was too afraid of herself to discard DNA proof just like that. It was painful to see her turn against herself. Slowly, I ran my finger along her jaw, lifting it up and kissing her. For a moment, her lips clung to mine.

'You don't want this, John. It's too late. I should never have left you in the first place...' She looked down at the floor, but I could hear that there was another burden in her voice.

'What is it, Scarlett? What is it you're not telling me?'

'I...John, you're going to hate me. I can't. I already can't look at myself in the mirror—'

'Please,' I interrupted her. 'There's nothing you can say that will turn me away from you. I read your file.'

Scarlett started clasping my face, my arms, my shoulders, as if I were a ghost. When she was sure I was not, she sighed with relief.

'Yes, I'm still here and I love you. There's nothing that will convince me otherwise.'

Scarlett hugged me tightly, kissing my cheek, but when she drew back again, I could see last traces of doubt in her eyes.

'If it helps, Scarlett, I have something to confess as well. Something I should've told you ages ago.'

She smiled at me forgivingly.

I took the leap. 'I cheated on you, Scarlett.' The word felt like lead in my mouth, but I forced them out all the same. 'Back at uni... I had noticed you were spending more and more time away from home. I thought you had someone else. But you didn't. And I didn't trust you. Then this girl came along – a first year, high-spirited and lovely. And she actually reminded me of you in happier times. I spent one night with her. That was it. Hated myself for it. But when I wanted to confess it to you, you had already found out – I still don't know how – and as I failed to mend our relationship, you did find someone else. You left me for him, and I couldn't blame you.'

Tears had filled Scarlett's eyes by now, but she was still smiling, shaking her head, relief in her breath.

'It's OK, John. I should've trusted you too,' she whispered, a rock was lifting off my chest.

I bit my lip and squeezed her hand, now myself trying to find out whether I was seeing a ghost. But her soft, cold skin was quite, quite real.

'All right,' I croaked when I had my voice back. 'Now it's your turn.'

She took a deep breath. 'John, I don't know why, but I still can't remember you, anything about us. Not even a glimpse of your face. All I remember is Eamonn and my victims.'

Now I could smile in relief. I had expected much worse. Of course, I was a bit crestfallen that she should remember such a monster over me, but then her memories of him were traumatic, which made them more likely to be triggered.

I drew her close to me and held her head. 'Don't worry. All in due time.'

A while later, the expert emerged from Sherlock's kitchen laboratory, declaring the charms were indeed genuine. Of course, they confiscated them. Lestrade now came in, scratching his head, to arrest Scarlett and Sherlock. I held Scarlett's hand until he was finished listing his horrible allegations. Then, they were cuffed and hauled off.

At the door, Sherlock briefly turned back to give me a slight, encouraging smile.

Mrs Hudson took my arm. 'What a dreadful business. I can't believe their nerve! But it will all turn out well. I'm sure of it, Dr Watson.'

37

I was startled at her using calling me this, just when Sherlock had done the same thing, but my surprise quickly vanished when the doors of the police car slammed shut.

'Well, it's nice to hear at least one of us is confident,' I remarked, straightening my body into my soldier's pose. My confidence would have to be won in battle now.

* * *

Lestrade took his time with the formalities, giving us some breathing space to brace ourselves. After that, Sherlock and I silently waited in our cell.

I missed John terribly. In all this chaos, I was desperate for someone to hold on to.

Sherlock noticed and took my hand, interlacing our fingers.

At last, I was called in for questioning.

'Don't say anything you don't know for sure, all right?' Sherlock advised me on my way out. 'I can prove you didn't commit those murders, and whatever you did in Bolivia doesn't concern the police here. D'you understand?'

I nodded, smiling.

He smiled back as encouragingly as he could.

Then, I was pulled out of his sight.

Fortunately, Lestrade himself was to interview me. He looked at me in the friendliest way, and I could see he would do all in his power to help. My files were lying on the table, and another constable by the name of Jones was to witness our conversation.

'Miss Vendalle,' Lestrade addressed me, placing photographs in front of me. 'We found traces of your blood on three of the victims. Evidence suggests you knew some of them. What is your connection between these people?'

I flinched as I seemed to recognise the faces. However, there were no memories of my talking to them. It was like I had seen these men, but only in static.

'I'm sorry. I don't know. I can't say if I ever met them before. You must excuse this. My memory still isn't fully recovered...'

'No worries, it's alright. I suggest you tell us all you know, and then we tell you all we found out.'

I gulped and nodded. After all I had seen, I had decided to tell them the truth. I felt painfully sorry for John and Sherlock's sakes that I should ruin all their efforts to protect me from the law, but I couldn't stand it anymore. If people were dying, if I had possibly killed them, I had to do everything to stop it. Some part of me knew I hadn't, but every other part of me told me I had better tell Scotland Yard it was me than risking their finding out the truth, whatever it was.

The deepest breath of my life – tip – plunge.

'At 221B, we've been getting strange messages for quite some time, and three weeks ago someone broke into our flat and chloroformed me in my bed. Sherlock and John weren't there at that time, I was alone. I didn't recognise the kidnapper – tall, broad man with tanned skin and black beard stubble. Big nose, dark eyes. He was wearing black all over. That's about all I can say. I tried to struggle, but he was fast and strong and I passed out before I had so much as scratched him. When I woke up, I was in some kind of underground office. No noise, no windows. After some time, Eamonn Doyle – a member of The Red Circle whom I met and fell in love with at university – came to me there. He was the reason I jointed the organisation but was ultimately betrayed. He tried to win my loyalty again. Eventually, he started torturing me so I would tell him what Sherlock had found out about him. I can't tell you how long he kept me down there, or where this could've been. Several times, I was unconscious, for

39

how long I don't know either. One day, he just gave it up. He forced me to drink something bitter and I passed out again. The next thing I knew was that someone must've brought me to a hospital, and John was with me. Please, believe me, this is all I know. If someone made me kill someone and wiped my memory afterwards, I cannot tell.'

Lestrade sat there, pondering for a long time. He was looking straight at me and I could tell that he believed me. But there was no way he could reconcile the evidence with my story. He exchanged an insecure glance with his constable, who raised his eyebrows, as clueless as the inspector.

Finally, Lestrade took *his* deepest breath. 'According to this file, you joined this... Red Circle eight years ago. You started out with several smuggling jobs, valuable goods, drugs and so on. After approximately a year, the organisation sent you to kill a man named Sholto. Can you confirm this?' He showed me the picture of the man with grey hair, whom I had remembered first when we'd been examining the body of Barker, a double agent Sherlock had been investigating. I could remember the screams now.

My throat painfully contracted as I opened my mouth. 'Yes, I can.'

Lestrade concealed his lips with his fist. He didn't know what to do. Finally, he spoke up again. 'So, according to this file, you killed 22 more people, all by order of this Eamonn Doyle. Only, he seems to have left the organisation by that time. Here, it says, "external order." Would you please take a look at the police reports? We couldn't find photos of everyone, as some seemed to have dodged the authorities themselves.'

Again, I could only confirm each assassination. With so many memories converging in my burning conscience, I was constantly at the edge of a panic attack, but managed to keep my composure somehow. Repentance, I thought.

'Did you know these people before you killed them?'

'I think some of them slightly,' I confessed.

'Why were you ordered to kill them?'

'Some of them were a threat to the organisation, had openly warned us they would expose The Red Circle, or had behaved suspiciously, so that Eamonn was convinced they would go to the police. Others had not delivered the goods we were expecting, or paid the money or ransom The Circle demanded. I couldn't tell which of those reasons Eamonn gave for each of them, though. It was long ago. You'll understand.'

Lestrade bit his lip. 'Yes, of course.' He paused for a moment, thumping through my files. 'But apparently, you weren't acting alone. There were two other assassins operating with you, besides Mr Doyle. Their names were Achmet James and Jenny Vandeleur.'

A flashbulb memory. They were sitting next to me, Jenny and Achmet. I heard cries and shots. Dust everywhere. I could barely recognise their faces. As if I had seen them only once before. Achmet was pressing a gun to my temple. Then another shot, blood gushing from his mouth. I shook my head.

'I remember them,' I said quietly. 'They were ambushed because of me.'

'But don't you remember more of them? Or of Eamonn Doyle?' Lestrade urged me. 'Scarlett, why did *you* commit these murders? I just can't imagine you did it just like that! Did anyone threaten you?'

I nodded, but didn't know why. The inspector's confidence in me filled me with warmth, but after a moment, tears started running down my cheeks as I found myself unable to retrieve the reason for my actions.

'There's nothing more I remember.'

'Maybe some more info will help,' Lestrade suggested, scanning the file once again. 'You mostly operated from La Paz, occasionally moving to Santa Cruz de la Sierra, Riberalta or El Sara. A few times, you seem to have smuggled "goods" across the border into Peru or Argentina, Brazil once. Does any of this ring a bell?'

I shook my head.

Lestrade sighed. Shuffling the papers again, he pulled out the list with the names of my victims. I read them carefully, but despite the pain in my gut, no more memories were triggered. I had to shake my head again.

Finally, Lestrade took another deep breath. 'Alright, there's one more thing in here – the codenames of you and your partners. Jenny Vandeleur apparently did a few jobs under the names of Beryl Stapleton, Mahomet Singh and Harry Staunton. Achmet James occasionally assumed the identity of Harold Latimer, Jonathan Small or J.W. Windle.' Lestrade threw a sceptical glance at me. He cleared his throat when I didn't react. 'There is only one alias of yours in the file: Mary Morstan.'

Cracks appeared in my view as my mind seemed to be torn apart.

Fragments. *That's all I am.*
Cutting edges of persons *I have forgotten.*
Puppets – angles – *strings*... cutting me...
Fragments cracking each other...
Burning ashes.
This is impossible.

My brain seemed to implode.
I forgot I ever had one life, but two.
Red silk.
Heavy skirt.
No escape.
Mary Boleyn.

Mary Morstan.

42

Chapter 4

'What!? What happened!?' I had picked up my phone. It was Lestrade. 'She confessed, John. I can't do anything for her.'

'But she couldn't have committed the murders and everything else was ages ago!'

'I know, John. It concerns the Bolivian authorities, not us, but she confessed so I'll have to keep her here until we know what to do.'

'Did she confess to the murders here, too?'

'Not yet, but she seemed to be willing to. I don't know what to say. There must be something behind this. It just seems odd, those files and everything. Like somebody wanted her to be convicted very badly.'

Lestrade's good nature seemed exasperated with the invisibility of criminality in people he knew. And yet, not once did he reproach us about having hidden an assassin from Scotland Yard. His good nature understood. Only to be more exasperated, of course, but the DI bore it with dignity.

'How is she?'

'She's resting now. Had some kind of fit while we questioned her, then passed out. We called a doctor. Nothing too serious, apparently. She woke up again after about half an hour, but hasn't spoken a word since. Or at least not that I know.'

'You tell me when she can speak again, d'you understand?'

'Of course.'

'And if she asks for me, please, let me see her.'

'I'll try. Alright, see you soon.'

'Yes. Bye.'

For a while, I listened to the Morse-like noises of the dead connection, then I covered my phone with my pillow.

Mrs Hudson kept me company while I desperately searched for any lead that could save Scarlett. The landlady even came along when I checked various hiding places which Sherlock and I had come to know over the years. Raum Q, the criminal hideout where we had first found Scarlett's file, was deserted as well. The search seemed hopeless.

Meanwhile, Sherlock's Irregulars were doing their best, but all they could find were clues about the planned robbery of the Crown Jewels. I even checked all *The Strand* issues we had collected for any clues about Scarlett or the Crown Jewels to find a connection, but there wasn't one. Scarlett's name appeared nowhere, as opposed to Sherlock's and mine.

Finally, I got help in the way I wanted the least. Our mysterious messenger paid us a visit and left a message in red paint on Mrs Hudson's window sill.

MEET HER AT WAKEFIELD TOWER   ED

Below the message there were three broken red threads. The third of the month. Whatever trap this might be, I was determined to risk it.

* * *

When I woke up in the middle of the night again, the full moon was shining bright, casting a pale light on the floor of our cell. It took me a while until I noticed that Sherlock was awake, too.

'What's keeping you up?'

'It's too bright in here. I can't sleep when there's light unless I'm high.' With a groan, the consulting detective sat up, supporting his chin with his folded hands, his legs tucked up.

'Alright, so... What are we plotting?'

'You shouldn't have confessed if you wanted to plot.'

'Once again, I'm sorry, Sherlock.' I looked away. Of course, he was right though. I observed him for a moment. 'But you *are* plotting, aren't you?'

'Yes.'

'Sorry, I haven't even asked yet. Is there any way I could help *you* get out of here? You *are* going to tell them I didn't confess to you, right?'

'I suppose so.'

Plotting silence. I could see by Sherlock's knitted brows that I had crossed his previous plans to an extent that had him rummaging around their crumpled shreds in his mental bin. Some pieces seemed to astonish him, but most of them gravitated right back to the rubbish pile.

'Listen, Sherlock, I know I shouldn't have done this. But I just couldn't live with myself, having done what I have done, and exploiting you and John on top of it. Those days in the cellar, they showed me what I really am. And you and John deserve better than that.' I bit back a sob.

Sherlock stared at the ground. 'John will forgive you.'

'And you?'

Silence. After a while, he slowly shook his head.

I didn't know what to say.

Sherlock just kept looking out of the window.

Then very, very slowly, he turned back to me, a clandestine smile stealing across his face.

'It was evident from the beginning that you would confess. That was the reason Eamonn Doyle locked you up in the first place. It wasn't about me or getting information at all. He knew that we knew about your past, and now he tried to make you remember enough to confess. From the first moment you came here, there were traces, clues of your past laid out for you. The red threads, the M and B charms, the Red Circle killing... I could go on and on. But something's still wrong about it. A man wouldn't want to get his revenge for an unhappy affair with that amount of effort. No, there must be something more. And I have a feeling I won't have to wait very long to figure it out.'

I couldn't suppress a sad smile. 'You still think you can save me, don't you?'

'Yes.'

'Will you tell John?'

Sherlock's lips twitched, his eyes blazing. A wordless pause filled with indescribable meaning.

I shook my head.

'You don't believe me.'

'I want to.'

'You'll see.'

'What makes you so sure?'

He didn't answer. For a long time, we sat in silence, looking at each other. With the moonlight shining through the window, Sherlock's skin seemed paler, his curls darker, holding more shadows than I had ever seen. The few spots touched by the light seemed almost ghostly.

Gazing out into the sky, Sherlock spoke again. 'When I met Irene, she'd been sentenced to death five times. Needless to say, she had escaped just as often. Maybe that was what attracted me to her. She kept dodging bullets that would've been impossible to miss. I don't know what went on in her head... One day, she got herself sentenced by a terror cell in the US. Something went wrong and I had to save her from being executed.'

'What happened?'

'A Mr Norton had betrayed her to the authorities, who were bribed to leak information on her whereabouts to the terror cell.'

'So, what did you do?'

'Well, you only have to say the right things to the right people. I went through the ranks until I had a seat in the front row. If I told you what actually happened then, I'd be giving away government secrets, but ask John; he might have accidentally heard something. When I had got Irene out of the crowd, we had someone sign her death certificate and went undercover for about a month under the names of Mr and Mrs Ashdown to avoid suspicion. You wouldn't believe how easily people will be fooled by married couples. Well, she got another name after that, and I managed to sneak back into England.'

I smiled at the story for a moment. 'Ashdown is a beautiful codename.'

Sherlock smirked. 'I got it from a 1970s detective film by an Austrian director. It was a flop, but I liked it.'

We both laughed.

'Sherlock, why did you never stay with Irene? She'd keep you in trouble, wouldn't she?'

Sherlock's lips forced a bittersweet smile on themselves. 'Mr Norton kept her in more trouble. She married him in the end. Besides, I couldn't leave John alone like this, not without someone like you.'

Once again, we found ourselves in silence for some time.

'I'm sorry, Sherlock.'

He shook his head.

'There is another reason you're telling me all this, isn't there?'

He smiled at my seeing through him. 'Irene's first codename was Lily Langtry.'

His shining grey eyes slowly, tenderly observed my face top to bottom. As the pictures in his mind seemed to become clearer, his gaze converged with mine, a remembering smile on his lips.

I clasped my mouth. So that's why he'd called me by my first name when he worried about me before. It had been a reflex.

After a moment, I gave him a coy smile. He looked out of the window. Unbelievable warmth radiated from his countenance. I slowly reached out and placed my hand on his. He closed his eyes with an imperceptible sigh. Suddenly, I had a notion.

Has he told me this story before?

Commotion in the corridor ripped us out of our thoughts. Sherlock stood up and stepped in front of me as the door to our cell was unlocked, and Lestrade came darting in.

'There's been another murder, Another member of The Red Circle, another message in blood. Please, tell me you can make something of this..'

He showed Sherlock a frayed note.

I looked over his shoulder.

Wake up the field agent
at Tower Bridge. He is
ready to go swimming.

Sherlock's eyes quickly jumped from line to line, scanning every corner of the note, then of his mind palace. His lips were moving silently. Lestrade helplessly looked between him and the note.

Something sounded familiar in these words...

'It's a skip code!'

'What?' Lestrade exclaimed.

Sherlock glanced at me, then back to the message. 'First word, then every third! You are brilliant!'

As he turned back to Lestrade, the detective inspector was already mumbling. '"Wake field Tower isgo?" What's that supposed to mean?'

'It's a plan. John told me you were with him when Hopkins died?'

Hopkins, one of Lestrade's former colleagues, had worked for Moriarty as a double agent before being killed off by his network one night I happened to sleepwalk around the Tower of London.

'Yeah, but what's *that* got to do with it?'

'You remember his dying words?'

'Of course. Something about... Wakefield Tower and the Crown Jewels!'

'Exactly. I suggest that if we go there now, we might be able to find out what they're up to. I suppose the fact that the murderer is still out there is proof enough that Scarlett is innocent?'

'I don't know,' Lestrade sighed. 'But I'll take it that way for now. Come on.'

Part 8: Spiral Palace

Chapter 1

It was a ghostly night. I spent hours shivering on the South Wall on Tower Hill, where Nora and Finch had helped me sneak in. Now, all we could do was wait.

As the clouds thickened above us, we heard steps some yards away from us, but couldn't make out more than a few fuzzy shadows. I waited for other sounds to emerge, but nothing happened for another hour. The wind became sharper as if it was whetting itself on our increasingly frozen noses. Eventually, the moon emerged from the clouds, and we saw ourselves breathing spectres.

For someone who hadn't spent hours in the dark without talking, it was utterly unimaginable how long it feels. Even I, who had been forced to do this by Sherlock in a considerable number of cases, was absolutely lost in time and space quite quickly. It didn't help to look at the watch. When the feeling in your extremities faded as well as the sense of time, one tended not to believe the things seen. For example, the hypothesis that my watch was frozen, as well as my nose - which I was expecting to fall off any moment like the one of the Great Sphinx of Giza - seemed much more logical to me than the fact that only another hour had passed.

Finally, a light appeared in the window of a tower opposite us. Nora excitedly nudged Finch and me when she spotted a crowd of fleeting shadows behind White Tower, coming closer and closer to us. There were about seven or eight of them. Some now entered Wakefield Tower through the door facing Tower Green, while the rest came dangerously close to seeing us as they entered the door facing the South Wall. One shadow kept guard outside.

* * *

Because Lestrade insisted, we had entered the Tower from the north and were now perched against the right wall of White Tower, facing the Jewel House. Lestrade was at the corner, while I was peering into the darkness from behind him with Sherlock as our rear guard. His coat billowed against my legs, and his leather-gloved hand on my upper arm prevented me from any sudden movements. The rest was pure cold.

Several shadows passed us, casting a biting breeze into our faces. Sherlock silently leapt out of his spot with feline swiftness and followed them as if he was one of them. My hand darted forward too late to hold him back.

Lestrade gave an angry start at Sherlock's disappearance, but because we were not shielded from the Jewel House by any barrier, he could not move out of the shadow or use his phone. Instead, he kept an eye on me and held me back whenever I felt an impulse to follow. I was touched by the inspector's concern, but angry that he was stronger than me.

With every passing figure, my desire to act became more unbearable.

The figures, however, did not touch Jewel House and soon vanished from our sight. Unfortunately, Lestrade had only left one junior officer at Wakefield Tower and he had preferred not to call his superintendent in feat that Sherlock would not have walked free so easily under his authority. Lestrade obviously preferred to rely on the consulting detective's help rather than on that of the superintendent, who had been Hopkins's superior.

Since there was no chance of calling anyone at all now, we were hopelessly outnumbered. I counted about fifteen dark shapes toward Wakefield Tower, and several more on the South Wall. Could any of them be John? It was just an inkling, but somehow, I kept imagining his short hair, brushed dark against the night sky. For a moment, I allowed myself to wonder what I would do if he were here. Keeping him out of trouble was my first instinct. I had to stop him from being arrested too, or worse – getting caught up in a fight with fifteen of Moriarty's men. My second was to apologise; my third to wrap myself up in his arms and kiss him.

A painful cry ripped me out of my thoughts. A cold suspicion that it was Sherlock's mercilessly gripped my brain. It seemed all of Moriarty's men were in Wakefield Tower now, so Lestrade called the Yard for support, then we both dashed into the building.

The large hall, to our surprise, was completely deserted. No sign of Sherlock or Moriarty's men. Instead, we found about a dozen security cameras staring at us from all directions. In the middle of the floor there were huge scratches in a strange shape. On approaching it, I could make out an octahedron. The exhibition on torture around the walls was still intact.

Lestrade exhaled heavily, rushing out of the other entrance.

The next moment, I could hear another heavy breath coming from the opposite direction. When I ran outside, I noticed someone following me from far behind, but before I could fully take heed of it, I saw Sherlock lying in the shadow next to Wakefield Tower. Blood was running down his left arm, and there was a nasty bruise on his forehead. He was a bit disoriented but not unconscious.

'Get up, go after them,' he hoarsely tried to urge me. 'They've got what they came for.'

'What happened?'

I spun around. My utter relief found John standing behind me. With raised eyebrows, he bent down and gave Sherlock a hand, who had no problem pulling himself up with his bleeding arm.

John noticed my surprise and remarked, 'It's his spare blood capsule. Apparently, he needed some sort of excuse for getting information out of someone, am I right, Sherlock?'

The consulting detective grinned with approving amazement. 'It would seem you knew my methods, John.'

'How come you're here?' I gasped. 'I hope you're not alone!'

'No, not at all.' He gestured at some direction in the darkness.

'Nora and Finch are with him. I told them to back him up, should he feel an urge to come to the Tower,' Sherlock explained.

'Yes, they ran over to the Jewel House just to check whether there's anyone in there. But I saw all fifteen that went into Wakefield Tower go out again at the opposite door,' John continued.

'It's no use! They've outwitted us this time. They must have transported the Crown Jewels into Wakefield Tower ages ago, and now they took them from there. But that's too simple! Oh, I can't believe this just happened right under our noses!' Sherlock angrily paced up and down, his fists clenched in his pockets.

'So, you saw the Jewels in Wakefield Tower?' I was astonished.

'No. Just them carrying off a large blue box, the size of a small room. Where's Lestrade?'

'He ran after them.'

Sherlock shook his head. 'He won't catch up to them. If he did, they'd shoot him, but I think he's well away from that danger.'

'Why don't we check the security cameras that were clearly meant to film this theft then?'

'Good idea. However Moriarty has tinkered with them, they'll tell us *something* about this whole affair.'

With some remote help from Toby, Sherlock's sniffer hacker, we were able to locate the device connected to the cameras in the North Bastion. The Gothic arches on the stone walls were an almost comic contrast to the dozens of plant pots and the neat garden bench lined up on either side of the front door.

'Sherlock, we can't just break in here, this is private accommodation,' John hissed. 'This is probably where the beefeaters live and they're all ex-military. I wouldn't be surprised if they still had an old weapon about.'

Sherlock just waved him aside. 'You're ex-military. You can have a chat. Veterans love other veterans, don't they?'

And with that, he picked the lock, strode in and disabled the burglar alarm. As quiet as two mice and a cat, we snuck up the stairs to a room with its door ajar, a flickering glow emerging from within.

'You can come in, Mr Holmes,' a muffled voice called from the room. It sounded like the man was eating something.

Sherlock grinned when John gestured at him angrily. 'What, did you think someone who would install a dozen cameras to watch the crime of the century doesn't have CCTV on his own front door?'

John scowled and we proceeded to the glowing room.

As we entered the room, we found a very round man in full beefeater uniform sitting at his desk with his back to us. In front of him were six computer screens, all split into four windows with footage from Wakefield Tower. A small buffet of snack bowls with odd foods in them, like sheep's trotters, dodgy smelling mince pies and shellfish were laid out on the desk – all items we had seen advertised in *The Strand Magazine* before. The man didn't turn around. Instead, he dipped one of his roasted sheep's feet in treacle and stretched out a meaty hand towards us. 'Aloysius Pork, pleasure to meet you.'

Sherlock did not shake the hand until it was retracted with a 'harumph' that sounded about as old as Queen Victoria herself. At first, none of us said anything as we observed the rest of the room. Mr Pork's walls resembled Sherlock's crime wall at Baker Street – except that there wasn't a single inch here which wasn't covered in sticky notes, photos, ticket stubs, small gauze pouches with tiny pieces of evidence, such as needles, buttons, hair, and hundreds of red threads were spun between pins.

Sherlock ran his fingers across the notes and pictures. 'You love your conspiracy theories, don't you, Mr Pork?'

'I beg your pardon!' the beefeater huffed, stuffing his face with a mince pie. 'I'll have you know I'm an amateur detective myself, Mr Holmes, just like you. Except I know how to avoid cameras. You didn't.'

'I wasn't trying to,' Sherlock said with disinterest. 'Mr Pork, all of your theories are completely and utterly…'

'I wouldn't say it if I were you,' Pork interrupted. 'This is my life's work.'

As I followed Sherlock's gaze, I realised that some of the photos seemed familiar. It took me a moment to realise Eamonn was looking down at me from every picture.

I blinked. There they were, his beady black eyes in every picture. I closed my eyes.

'You're obsessed with this man, aren't you?' Sherlock shot Pork a glance.

The beefeater swivelled comfortably in his wooden chair. 'Not one man.' He swung around to grin at us. 'Several. It's a double bluff. You see, everyone who comes in here assumes this is one and the same person in multiple disguises. I tell you it's several people playing the same part. Have a think about that.'

We all stared at the pictures, but couldn't, or didn't want to follow his train of thought. There was something far more sinister in what he'd said than even he seemed to realise.

The silence lay heavily on Sherlock until eventually, he approached Pork. Looking at the beefeater's face, I felt like his large nose and Victorian whiskers might be an attempt to conceal his identity, but his voice was in no way like Eamonn's; it was higher-pitched and raspier.

Sherlock cocked his head as he, too, seemed to consider ripping off the man's mask. 'Mr Pork, I seem to have underestimated you. What can you tell us about the robbery of the Crown Jewels?'

Aloysius Pork wiped the sweat off his brow with a white handkerchief. 'The what of the what?'

'What you've just been watching on your 24 feeds of live footage there, my good man.'

'Oh, it was really boring actually. Absolutely nothing happened until you bumbled through the shot for no reason.'

This was too much for John. 'You must have seen something! Did you put up all those cameras? Did you manipulate the footage so the thieves could get away? Out with it, you pretentious swine!'

'I find that last word very inappropriate considering,' replied Mr Pork, somewhat intimidated, 'I really don't know what you're talking about. You tell me why you broke into the premises at night and how you found out the cameras were mine!'

'We didn't break in, we were asked to be here by the police,' Sherlock said calmly. 'You can let him go, John, he's telling the truth.'

'Then how did he know your name before we even entered this room? And what's all that about the crazy stuff on the walls and...'

'Alright, alright, I am a bit of a fan,' admitted the man. 'I saw your cases in *The Strand*, and always wanted to be a detective myself. Then I find all these men dressing up as the same person, some of them wearing prosthetics, others just using makeup or choosing a completely different look but the same gaze… One by one, they seemed to start popping up around the Tower of London, and here I was, at the heart of a mystery! So, methinks, I'll put together all the clues, until one of these men even goes on a tour through the Tower with me, but escapes every single security camera in some freak way. So, here I am setting a trap in one of the towers where you absolutely cannot escape the CCTV, add a few more cameras for good measure, just testing them out now before I run another tour tomorrow, and who do I see but my favourite detective walking into my trap with his trusty sidekick and a bunch of strangers.'

'I'm not a sidekick,' John growled, but Sherlock gestured for him to be silent.

'Did you not see the police on any of the other CCTV?' I asked.

'I ain't got access to that,' said the beefeater. 'This is my own kit. Thought I could finally convince my colleagues that these photos were of different men. The number of bets we've got going on! Anyway, did the police catch him? I hope they did. I just want proof now.'

'You don't happen to have any copies of *The Strand* on you?' Sherlock spoke even more slowly than before.

'Oh no, burnt them all after reading,' Mr Pork grinned proudly at us.

'Shame, I would have left you an autograph. Thank you for your time, Mr Aloysius Pork.'

And with that, John and I found ourselves scrambling after the infamous detective. As the door closed with a loud creak behind us, Sherlock gave us instructions:

'John, collect Nora and Finch, we need to get to the Yard.'

'I think so, too, Mr Holmes.'

Wincing at the voice, we turned around. So, Lestrade *had* called his superintendent after all. I felt sorry for him. Before I could feel sorry for us though, Sherlock murmured 'Vatican Cameos!' and together he and John jumped at the policeman.

At first, my heart leapt up with joy at our easy escape, but only a few moments later, the beefeaters living in the houses next to us, roused by one of their colleagues, came pouring into the courtyard. I made for the nearest entrance into Wakefield Tower, grabbing John's hand. When Sherlock didn't join us, we took another route back onto the South Wall. Running across it, we could see him being cuffed and escorted away before we ran into Nora and Finch.

'We only jus' made i'. Sherlock ran straigh' into their arms. We couldn' do anythin' for 'im!' Nora cried angrily.

'I think 'e migh' 'ave wan'ed the police to feel some success, so they'd leave us alone. E did tha' before for us,' Finch explained, though he didn't look happy about it either.

'That was before my time,' John stated with a heavy sigh.

* * *

It was very difficult to try and stop Scarlett from running straight back to the police. Only a very long, arduous argumentation and some brandy could convince her that she wouldn't help Sherlock by getting herself arrested again. A more elaborate plan was needed, and I had the ingenious idea of asking for Mrs Hudson's help.

'Of course, dear, I'll just get some biscuits and tea,' she agreed as if I had suggested a knitting session. The woman was simply heaven-sent.

A moment later, she ooh-ed herself into our living room, sitting down in Sherlock's armchair opposite Scarlett who had wrapped herself in a blanket like a human-sized burrito.

'I've got a plan already, dear, don't you worry. Help yourself to a cuppa, and everything will be fine,' she addressed us warmly, holding out two steaming cups.

Scarlett gratefully took hers. 'Thank you, Mrs Hudson. I trust your plan is as good as your tea.'

The old lady smirked cheekily. 'Oh, naturally, my dear, naturally. You wouldn't believe the situations I had to wriggle myself out of when I was young. I got so used to it, one might say I danced out of trouble in my prime, if you know what I mean.'

I shook my head. This certainly wasn't the time to listen to an old lady's indecent escapades.

'We need to do something as soon as possible, as much as we'd love to hear your anecdotes.'

'Well, I can only say you're missing out, but believe it or not, I wasn't planning on telling you the adventure of the bankrupt bar, or the puzzled policeman. I know exactly what you need to do, and it's not what Sherlock told me to tell you.'

Now, I was steaming with anger that he was even trying to tell us what to do when he wasn't there. Nonetheless, I enquired what he had said.

'Oh, to leave him alone, he had it all under control, and such nonsense. That's what you men always think,' sneered the landlady.

'I have to clear John of that charge, Mrs Hudson. He never knows what's going on, and he's wise enough to admit it,' Scarlett remarked with a broad grin.

I palmed my face. 'Can you please let me know what *is* going on then, if you know everything better than me?'

Scarlett apologetically squeezed my hand, and Mrs Hudson handed me an excusing biscuit. 'What we need is getting Sherlock out of prison as soon as possible. I understand there is enough evidence to keep him at the constabulary for a considerable amount of time, so waiting is not an option. I assume clearing him won't be easily possible either?'

I shook my head. 'It's not like passing off drugs as herbal soothers when the sergeant comes to relieve you of some tea and biscuits, Mrs Hudson.'

'As I thought... So, the only option remaining is to help him escape. By the time we get there, he would probably have started digging a hole with a spoon, anyway, so the sooner we save him the trouble, the better.'

'I rather think he'd manipulate the guards,' Scarlett noted.

'Just as effective in some cases,' Mrs Hudson waved her aside. 'Anyway, my plan is to drive to the constabulary, whichever one it is that that superintendent sits in, and to tell him of the robbery in my flat.'

'The what!? You're just making this up, aren't you?' I exclaimed incredulously.

'Oh, it's not a big deal. They only stole an old clock of mine, hideous thing, but I inherited it from my father, so I could never get rid of it. Whoever took it must have felt the same about it, because the next day I found it at the front door. They should've kept it, because now it's stopped working, but I haven't had the time to dispose of it yet. Maybe I won't. Anyway, I'll pretend I want to find out who broke into my house. Then I will give them some special biscuits with a nice dose of my herbal soothers in them. And finally, we'll use Sherlock to tell us where the key to his cell can be found. If we leave a recording of Sherlock muttering in his cell, it'll take them a while to realise something's wrong after I dealt with them. We'll take my car.'

A proud smile spread over our landlady's face.

The night was beginning to lighten as we drove to Sherlock's rescue. Mrs Hudson's plan seemed foolproof. Of course, nothing went to plan in the end, as anything involving Sherlock Holmes, but what else were we to do?

When we arrived at the constabulary, we were told they were holding Sherlock under suspicion of several offences, some of which he had already confessed to. 'We just finished questioning him. He's in his cell. Frankly, I didn't expect him to have so many visitors so late at night.' The sergeant scratched his head. 'But we couldn't deny a damsel in distress to see her husband when she heard he'd been arrested.'

Mrs Hudson, Scarlett and I must have looked like a herd of sheep. The sergeant laughed uneasily.

'Well, what can I say... I'm not sure you're too welcome altogether, but should I show you over nonetheless?'

None of us managed more than a nod, so the sergeant led the way.

'I told you everything will be fine, my darling,' Sherlock's soothing voice echoed from the walls of the corridor when we approached the cell. *What a weird thing for him to say...*

'But how are we to go on our holiday? Everything is spoilt!' A dramatic female voice wailed.

Irene Adler! It couldn't be!

Before the sergeant opened the door for us, I knew this was a prank. I was offended.

'This can't be! Boss!' The sergeant stormed out of the empty cell, only to reveal a smartphone playing a wonderfully acted parody of Sherlock and Irene's relationship.

'Well, I think we can conclude that Mrs Hudson is as smart as Irene Adler. Any relation there?' I asked, trying to lighten the mood.

'It's a compliment, Mrs Hudson, believe me,' Scarlett assured the slightly annoyed landlady.

'Well, what now?' Mrs Hudson pursed her lips.

'We can't leave him with Irene,' I maintained. 'He might like her, but I don't. Let's go!'

'John, calm down.' Scarlett put her hand on my arm. 'Where would you go?'

'To find them, what do you think?'

'Exactly, and in order to do that, you need to know where they are. We just need to read the clues they've left us here.'

'But, but, what?' I stammered, but Scarlett had already jumped into the cell and was looking at the phone they had left.

'They're still here,' she exclaimed, hopping out of the cell and up and down the corridor. 'Now we only need to search the building for an unoccupied room without cameras.'

I understood nothing and had to run after someone speaking cryptically. *Gosh, this really is just as if Sherlock was here!*

'What makes you say all that, Scarlett? How could you possibly—'

'Bluetooth.'

'What?' Mrs Hudson was panting behind me.

A herd of policemen including the superintended rushed past us, back to the cell. When they were gone, Scarlett explained, still running in front of us:

'The file the phone was playing had been transferred to it only two minutes ago, Bluetooth was still turned on, and the device that transferred the file is still available for sharing with this one.'

Mrs Hudson and I shared a glance. 'Where are we heading then?'

'They must be in a room that doesn't have CCTV, otherwise security would have spotted them already. Now, there are exactly two rooms that don't usually need surveillance: the lavatories, and the superintendent's office. Where do you think Sherlock will choose to be?' Scarlett smirked.

A pompous sign on one of the more remote doors showed us which room to enter. To both my relief and my annoyance, Scarlett had deduced completely correctly.

'I told you to turn off Bluetooth, amateur,' Irene grumbled at our arrival.

'Lovely to see you, too, Irene,' I replied.

'Indeed,' Sherlock confirmed. 'I think that might be why I left it on...'

Scarlett grinned. Irene sighed.

Sherlock jumped off the superintendent's desk. 'Shall we?'

We needed no second invitation. Like on cue, we dashed down the corridor, down the stairs and squeezed into Mrs Hudson's car, who was, by now, steaming with anger, but I seemed to be the only one to notice.

After driving a few miles away from the constabulary in a random direction, she stopped by the side of a lonely road and coolly smiled at Irene and held out an open tin.

'Biscuits, anyone?'

I had to try hard to suppress a grin. Scarlett looked the other way.

'Oh, that's odd,' replied Irene, with no intention of taking anything from a strange old lady.

To my astonishment, Sherlock assured her as he reached for the tin himself, 'You can trust her, Mrs Hudson's biscuits are the best in London.' The next moment he swallowed one himself.

That convinced Irene.

I inconspicuously parked my hand in front of my mouth.

How long will it take for the biscuits to take effect?

'Now, please get out of my car, Miss,' commanded Mrs Hudson all of a sudden.

Irene nearly spat out the biscuit.

'Well, thank you for your generosity,' she retorted sarcastically, waving me out of the way.

I opened the door and got out to let her exit as I'd been sitting next to her in the back. But when Irene stepped out, I could see she'd been typing away on her phone behind her back. A moment later something stung my neck, and the sun stopped dawning.

Chapter 2

'John!' I rushed out of the car, so did Mrs Hudson, only to hold me back. Within five seconds, Irene had drugged John with a syringe, thrown it in our faces and put a tiny gun to his temple.

'One more step, and he dies. You know I don't care about him,' Irene bluffed.

Sherlock was already asleep in the back of the car, thanks to Mrs Hudson's unsavoury biscuits. I was wondering how Irene was holding up so well, but waiting didn't seem to help at all. There we were in a standoff with only one side armed. I grew angrier and angrier at my inability to act, but Mrs Hudson had a firm grip on me. My fingers twitched aimlessly in the air for a trigger that wasn't there.

I didn't even know what to say. Mrs Hudson tried to reason with Irene, naturally without success, but I was too numb to even register. We should have seen it coming that the woman was expecting back up. Irene was beginning to seem drowsy when a vintage Rolls Royce pulled up next to her, dropping a smoke bomb. And gone she was, taking John away.

With a scream of frustration, I kicked Mrs Hudson's expensive car. The old lady winced, but didn't say anything. She just got in and hit the accelerator once I was inside as well, racing after them. The road was empty, straight and lonely for some miles, not a single road meeting it. In any case, the car had just vanished in that cloud of smoke. I was utterly devastated. It felt like a leaden bell that rang in my deafened ears whenever I moved my head. I couldn't even close my eyes when Anne sat down on my lap. She was just a little child. I welcomed her company. She smiled at me and reached for my face with her little hands…

Suddenly, I saw a red line with stitches around her neck. Her face was white as death, and her hands grew rigid. Before I could react, she

ripped off my head and

looked down at it.

I could do nothing
but stare at her face from

below.

Then, the little girl
tore the threads on her neck…   the vivid thread of life…

And placed her head
on my neck.

With a laugh, she tried to put my head
on her body, with my hands…

But it couldn't carry me. It tumbled off…

I woke up again when we arrived at Baker Street. Together, Mrs Hudson and I carried Sherlock up the stairs, but then realised we needed Mycroft's help.

'I'm so sorry, dear, I wish we could avoid talking to this bastard, pardon me, but I think we're out of our depth here…' Mrs Hudson sighed.

Yet the spectacle awaiting us in the living room made us forget all the plans we'd had. All the furniture was Victorian. Brand new as if we'd just bought it. And so was the dark red wallpaper, the newspapers, any papers we could get our hands on.

On top of that, all the electronic devices were gone. A single gas lamp cast a dingey light on the terrible change that had overcome the flat, flickering as if it was laughing at us madly. This was too much.

Mrs Hudson rushed down the stairs, and seconds later she came back in, dragging Mycroft by his ear. 'You are telling us what's going on here right now. You say you're smarter than Sherlock – go on, prove it!'

Mycroft wasn't even awake properly, but he was certainly scared of Mrs Hudson. When he finally realised what was wrong, he squinted twice. Then he sighed.

'Not that too…'

We begged him to explain, but he didn't say a word until we were all seated in the kitchen with *a candle* and some tea we had to boil with fire.

'I've been trying to keep Sherlock safe from this.' He sighed again. 'It's true. All is true. As far as I can see at least. It began a few years ago. I had always tried to retain the position of Sherlock's archenemy, but like every love affair, it got old. You will have heard the name James Moriarty, I presume. It was around the time my brother first met him. Of course, Sherlock, shall we say, "fancied" him over me, and you might do the same if I asked you who succeeded me in my position. However, this is not what happened. Sherlock suddenly had a much more powerful opponent.

'Like you, I first came across an old *Strand Magazine*. One of the members of the Diogenes club – Douglas Wilmer– had left it behind accidentally. I was curious, because it surprised me such an old thing, issued July 1891, was still in one piece. Naturally, such illustrated magazines are usually beneath me, but when I thumbed through the pages, my brother's name suddenly stared me in the face. I know mother has a strange taste in baby names, and so did the Victorians, but this – a coincidence? The universe is hardly so lazy. It got even better when I found the word 'detective' appearing suspiciously often, sketches appeared that resembled my brother – though his good looks were overdone somewhat – and last but not least the name Irene Adler.

'This woman had appeared in the tightest spots the secret service has had the misfortune of finding itself in. But in an old magazine, with my brother? I can hardly blame myself for reading the story, and taking every step to find any evidence that the magazine was a fake. But, like my little brother, I failed to. And I am by far his superior in these things. A few weeks later, disaster struck and my brother *met* Irene Adler. One of my men had not been careful enough and permitted a client to get in touch with Sherlock over some trouble regarding precarious photographs. I couldn't believe what I heard, but before my eyes, as it has done before yours, the story unfolded. I don't *like* to admit it, but I cannot pretend to have left out any attempts at steering the plot, even some quite foolish ones. The result was that my brother got even more infatuated with a woman that was clearly dancing on my nose, and there was nothing I could do.

'Eventually, I decided to "keep calm and carry on" as the phrase goes. To no avail, of course. My research resulted in alarming findings. Soon enough, more Sherlock Holmes stories started appearing in an old digital archive. After nearly every new case he solved that hadn't been in a story previously, I found a new, corresponding adventure in *The Strand Magazine*, the records of Arthur Conan Doyle's sensational publication increasing, and the illustrations of my brother getting more accurate. Naturally, Sherlock started to suspect me the more I tried to oppose this horrible enemy, and I decided it was best for him if he never saw what I had seen. I knew it would drive him mad, and I tried to protect him. So, I deleted all records I discovered.'

'You did *what!?*'

'I blocked the stories from the web, and with them all information concerning Sherlock Holmes. Even had to take down his website. He's been so busy he didn't even notice,' Mycroft sneered. 'Oh, yes, and I had that theatre lady abducted, Mrs Lynch, if I remember correctly, from the Duchess.'

I gave him a hard stare. 'Next, you'll be telling me you bribed that criminal St Clair to kill off the poor ticket seller in Regent's Park!'

We had tried to speak to the little man in Victorian clothing before he was shot out of nowhere.

'I had to do it! You've seen the consequences!' Mycroft defended himself. 'If you had seen it happen, would you have let your sister believe she was only a character in a story?'

What did he say? My sister? He meant brother, surely...

Once again, my head began to whirl, but Mrs Hudson caught me. Her grip on my shoulder was firm.

'There's more,' the old landlady's voice rang out harshly.

I was astonished at first, but then I too realised Mycroft's ear twitching and the slightest drop of sweat on his temple. He could not escape Mrs Hudson now.

'There are... adaptations,' he finally gurgled.

Mrs Hudson pursed her lips. 'I hope I appear in them at all!'

Mycroft was more than uncomfortable now. He had clearly seen several impersonations.

'How did you find this out?' I asked him.

'There was an article in the December 1915 issue of *The Strand*. I found it in my decanter at the Club. It was titled "Stranger than Fiction," written by now "Sir" Arthur Conan Doyle. He was relating coincidences in life, so strange that he suggested some higher force to be at work. Utter nonsense most of it, of course, but you know my opinion of coincidences. So, I researched what he was claiming of a man under the false name "Wilder", which Doyle had given him for privacy reasons.

'Merely googling, I stumbled across an Austrian director of that name, who apparently had earned enormous fame in Hollywood. Naturally, this being a false name in the article, I was looking at the wrong man, but when I scrolled down the page, once again my little brother's name suddenly jumped out at me from the screen. The *private life* of him, no less... The idiot director had made a film about it before my brother was even born. Of course, the actor they'd cast – something Stephens was his name – did not look nearly like my brother, but he was vain enough to nail the part. I couldn't believe my eyes. I stopped watching when, well, *I* entered the screen, played by none other than Dracula himself, who would believe it...'

Mrs Hudson and I glanced at each other and burst out laughing, only stopping when Mycroft gave us a withering look.

'There was a red-headed woman in it, too, by the name of Gabrielle Valladon. She appeared to have fallen in the Thames and lost her memory before being brought to Baker Street.'

I must have looked very sheepish that moment as Mycroft seemed to struggle to conceal an impish smirk. His stiff upper lip won, however, and he proceeded:

'Likelihood suggests there are more adaptations, but I have so far managed to avoid the embarrassment of finding another one. I only beg of you to keep this secret from Sherlock – his ego will go through the roof, and I'm sure Mrs Hudson would like to keep damage to the house at a minimum.'

We laughed again. Mycroft did not.

It was hard to consider this seriously, but then I recalled that Sherlock himself had mentioned a 1970s film by an Austrian director that he had taken his alias "Ashdown" from. Sure enough, when we looked it up, it was indeed featured in The Private Life of Sherlock Holmes as an alias the detective used himself. I remembered Sherlock had said he liked the film. What a cynical statement in the end.

For a time, we tried to figure out how Sherlock had come by the film, how much he may have known, or who could have planted it on him, but all traces had been removed expertly. Eventually, we decided to forget about the film and follow other leads, just as something else began tampering with our lives.

* * *

You will kill him!
You will writhe and you will squirm, but you will do as I say. You will get sick of him. He will drive you mad. You will not be able to live with him.
You will have to kill him.
He is wasting my life, your life. I have important work to do, a legacy to leave. If in 100 years I am only known as the man who invented Sherlock Holmes, then I will have considered my life a failure. And you will relieve me of him. Because you are me, John Watson.

It was hard to explain what really happened. I could not trust my senses or memory. I was clearly hallucinating, except hallucinations didn't make sense, and mine did. At the end. The end of the story. And for me, there was nothing left to do but to tell it.

When I woke up – if I ever did – I couldn't see. I didn't know where I was, how long I had been unconscious, in short – the usual when a criminal abducts you and they aren't an amateur. This situation didn't alarm me. I had been in worse positions and when it came to escaping them, I was second at weaselling out only to the actual animal... And Sherlock.

That bastard. Why had he eaten Mrs Hudson's biscuits!?

'You idiot!' I tried to shout.

It only took me a few moments to realise no sound had come from my lips. I could feel nothing stopping me from shouting though. I hadn't been gagged, and my ears felt untouched.

Did they paralyse me?

Suddenly, the darkness felt familiar. It was oppressive. Before my eyes, it seemed to coil up into swirls that pervaded my brain. I stopped breathing for fear of gas, but the swirling continued, and stars appeared which I could only drive away by breathing again. Apart from my own breath, I soon realised, I could perceive no sound. And this was exactly what frightened me when suddenly a voice appeared in my head:

You will writhe and you will squirm, but you will do as I say. You will get sick of him. He will drive you mad. You will not be able to live with him.

There were no headphones on me, no perceivable source of this sound at all, and no second breath. Only mine. When the voice had repeated *You will kill him!* for the third time, I felt my lips move and my voice followed.

You will kill him!
You will writhe and you will squirm, but you will do as I say. You will get sick of him. He will drive you mad. You will not be able to live with him.
You will have to kill him.
He is wasting my life, your life. I have important work to do, a legacy to leave. If in 100 years I am only known as the man who invented Sherlock Holmes, then I will have considered my life a failure. And you will relieve me of him. Because you are me,
John Watson.

71

The only perceivable source was me. The power over my body and mind had left me. For the moment, my hands and legs were tied quite literally anyway. I tried to convince my limbs to wriggle free or move at all, not knowing that the danger would only begin when I was cut loose.

* * *

Sherlock woke up on the floor just about when Mycroft had finished his speech. Nobody felt like divulging it to him. He did deduce we had just dropped him at the sight of the flat and kindly forgotten him while Mycroft had been telling fancy tales. He also didn't blame us. Of course, Sherlock had his brother thrown out again as fast as he could stumble over his umbrella.

'Now we're waiting for hansom cabs to appear in the street, are we?' I said after a while, to lighten the mood, but Mrs Hudson only shuddered, and Sherlock dryly pointed out there was one right across the street.

He wasn't joking.

I felt quite the idiot.

There was a really long, awkward pause. Mrs Hudson went to make another fire to boil more tea. As Sherlock started going through his possessions, he slowly shook his head. His elbow was perched on his left hand while his right was reaching out to support his head, but had stopped halfway.

Five minutes later, he was still shaking his head. I doubt he noticed the cup of tea Mrs Hudson had placed into his floating hand. She looked very worried.

'Sherlock,' she began. He didn't react. 'Try to stop thinking about all this. I don't mind my flat being Victorian, but John needs your—'

'I don't need anyone telling me what to do! I know what happened! Now will you please shut up and let me figure out how to find him!'

Thinking of John, I felt a sudden sting in my gut. Looking for help, I shot a glance out of the window, in the hope that he was merely a few feet away from home.

Chapter 3

I cannot remember moving away from the window for the next two days. There must have been something in the tea Mrs Hudson had made me.

Sherlock had no time to question it, however. Or maybe he didn't deem it necessary. Instead, he did everything in his power to find out any hint as to John's whereabouts, and so did the now Victorian Irregulars. They had woken up in different clothes one morning, it seemed, but weren't sure if they'd ever owned any others. Fog was creeping through the city, they said, and if they ever had a life in a different time, the fog had taken it.

Whenever Sherlock or one of the Irregulars came home from yet another hopeless mission, I could hear him muttering under his breath as he found a letter on his doorstep each time. These usually contained the knowledge of where Sherlock had been and a warning that he would find John in *his own time*, or else he would die.

Sherlock didn't stop, of course.

When I finally felt myself capable of moving again, I found myself in a different conundrum. Lestrade appeared several times at our door 'trying' to arrest us, while actually clearly trying to prove we were not at home. Sherlock being on a frantic search for John unfortunately did not give him brain space to hide, so Mrs Hudson and I had to cover up for him (*and the Victorian flat*) in front of Lestrade's colleagues.

We were beginning to welcome this task as distraction from all the misery we couldn't escape when eventually the day came – the day Sherlock had tried everything.

On getting out of the shower, I perceived a sound completely unexpected: Sherlock playing his violin. He hadn't in ages. Perhaps this was his only refuge from the fear tearing him apart. John had been gone for five days now, and it seemed there was nothing we could do that wouldn't kill him. Except playing the violin... And yet, I was afraid something might happen.

Is there a code in his song, anything conveying meaning that could set off a bomb wherever we wouldn't expect it?

I didn't know. I didn't know the song at all. Knowing Sherlock though, I knew he had composed it. He had a very distinct style, sweeping melodies with ecstatic highs inevitably followed by heavy lows.

The sound was mesmerising. The wild leaps in his tunes had absolute power over me. With only my towel wrapped around me, I stepped into the living room. Sherlock's fine, vibrating notes were chasing each other through the room, turning into sparks on my skin. I slowly approached him. He was standing at the window, the curtains drawn, the best of targets.

What is he doing?

The melodies seemed to sadden more and more as I came closer. When I laid my hand on his shoulder at the end of a phrase, he paused on the highest note, the most beautiful fermata. We held the tone in the air for ages, deafening the silence that followed his song.

Suddenly, a chair creaked, and the bubble burst – the tone was dead.

Sherlock took down the violin and looked at me over his shoulder. His eyes were deep, cold, and desperate, like a well he was about to drown in. I laid my hand on his cheek.

His eyes grew deeper.

'You should get dressed,' he murmured.

'I know,' I whispered, without moving.

Sherlock cautiously turned around to me.

'I'm sorry. I shouldn't be so careless,' he said softly, his deep voice resonating in my mind in its unforgettable way. I gave him a forgiving smile. I knew he was wondering whether life would be worth living without John. I nearly broke at the thought myself. It certainly wouldn't be worth very much...

'John would probably forbid your thoughts if he saw you like this,' I insisted.

Sherlock replied, 'He would certainly forbid yours.'

My gaze softened even more together with his.

Suddenly, he said, 'Allow me to forbid them for him.'

Hit by a wave of empathy, I swallowed all my regrets. The next moment, I felt myself cling to Sherlock's neck, my bare skin against his clothes, my wet hair at his cheek. He carefully put the violin out of his hand, and to my astonishment returned my embrace. His cold hands were yet warmer than my drying hair, as he wrapped his fingers around my neck. His other arm was gently placed around my waist to keep me from falling down. For a moment, he quietly, almost imperceptibly swayed me to and fro. I was the only piece connecting him to John, and he was the only in mine. All the inexplicable events of the last few days kept wreaking havoc in our minds, shaking us out of our wits, and for this one moment, we were shaking in synchrony.

'It will be all right. I promise,' he murmured into my ear, his hand clutching my shoulder. It was warm now.

In the face of the vanity of this promise, I bowed my head and buried it in his chest. I knew I would never forget his lips on my hair the next moment. It was nothing more than a kind gesture of comfort, but I could feel his guilt as well.

There was nothing we could do.

* * *

He will take her from you! Did you ever doubt that? He is not your friend! He needs you because you are useful to him. That is not friendship.

I was quite aware that the voice in my head was trying to manipulate me, so I kept fighting it, no matter what mantra it made me say over and over again.

I trusted Sherlock. I trusted Scarlett.

I knew trust wasn't worth much.

The question of how I had come here, why no one was coming to rescue me, how they could have been so careless, how they could be so careless now, started forcing itself onto my mind with ever increasing insistence.

I still couldn't see or hear, and my hope of someone entering the room to ask me questions, give me food or at least torture me had completely vanished now.

Of course, sleep was a luxury I could not hope to even be overcome by.

How they were keeping me alive, I do not know.

* * *

As we stood there at the window, both Sherlock and I were hoping to be arrested. If John died, we knew it was our fault entirely.

Sherlock had spent day and night following every lead, but if it was anyone who could not excuse themselves through incapability it was him. In fact, he had been so unlike himself all day that I suspected he was hiding something from me. I could not help but wonder if he'd found a new story in *The Strand Magazine* that told him John was dead.

'Sherlock, what changed today? You didn't find another magazine, did you?'

'Yes...' It sounded like he was cutting into his own throat with his voice.

'Why didn't you tell me?'

'It isn't important,' he grunted through his teeth.

'But what if it helps us to find John? What if it's meant to lead us somewhere?'

'It's not. At least not to John...' Sherlock's voice trailed away from time and space, giving me a shudder. These moments of utter defeat had become dangerously frequent in his mind.

'How can you be so sure?'

'I know what's going to happen now.'

'What? Is John safe?'

'Yes.'

'Do you really think you can trust that magazine?'

'I don't think that I have a choice. But that's beside the point.'

'What *is* the point then, Sherlock?' I was getting more and more unnerved.

'I cannot and will not elaborate,' he barked, stiffening his upper lip as if he had just crossed a creaking threshold. 'We will receive news about Watson soon, I think. The game is afoot.'

'Did you really just say afoot?'

'Did I?'

'Come on, you can't be serious.'

'Never mind the wording. The fact is we are going to be led into a trap to save John, and no, that's not in the magazine, but we are *going* into that trap. I don't care what's waiting for us there. I only know time's running out, and it's just grown an extra pair of legs.'

And with that cryptic sentence, Sherlock's face froze and there was not another word I could get out of him.

Before our eyes, thick fog emerged. At first, I thought it was merely in my mind, but when I allowed my perception to overcome the filters of my brain, I started in shock. The opposite building had vanished entirely. Sherlock opened the window, but nothing changed. The fog only ceased in the evening when Mrs Hudson had brought us a cup of tea again. As the view came back through our window, Sherlock began to smile.

The whole street had changed. Every trace of the 21st century had disappeared. By the time I shook myself out of my stupor, Sherlock had discovered something. He was standing in the kitchen motionlessly, once again not drinking his cup of tea. I carefully walked over to him and glanced around his shoulders.

UPPER BAKER ST LONDON NW

'Why hasn't he signed it this time?' was the first question that found its way out of my mouth and into the room.

'Because this time, it's not from Eamonn Doyle. Since you remember *him* already, you should see the difference.' He was silent for a moment.

I tried hard to overcome my feeling of guilt. 'Who is it from then?'

'Trust me, you don't want to know. Mrs Hudson!?'

A nervous cluttering could be heard from the living room. A second later, the landlady scuttled into the room.

'Oh!' she exclaimed. 'Another one?'

Her voice was too high-pitched. Something was very wrong.

'Scarlett, fetch my coat,' Sherlock said gravely. 'The Victorian one. There'll be a dress in your room, I presume.'

I nodded wordlessly and went upstairs. Indeed, there was an extremely beautiful dress of a sombre, grayish beige, untrimmed and unbraided, and a small turban of the same dull hue, relieved only by a suspicion of white feather in the side. Without being able to question how it had found its way into my room or my ownership of it, I put it on. It fit me perfectly, as if I had been wearing it for years. Suddenly, I could not have imagined wearing anything other than dresses like this one.

With perfect skill, I wound up my hair in Victorian fashion and crowned it with the turban.

When I came downstairs, the door to the flat was open.

'Mrs Hudson has gone out. I wouldn't follow her if I were you. We're going to find Watson now. Are you ready?'

I coyly entered the living room. Immediately, Holmes's eyes were riveted to me as if he remembered me from a former life. I seemed to hear him murmur:

'I have never looked upon a face which gave a clearer promise of a refined and sensitive nature.'

'I beg your pardon?' I frowned.

'Watson's words. His diary…' Holmes replied, immersed so visibly, so deeply in his thoughts about the story, I feared he would disappear into it. Besides, he was right. I could hear John's voice in his words. We had but to follow them.

When we were out in the street, Holmes explained, 'Someone is trying to help us, which means it's a trap.'

'Wait, do you think it meant John was in Baker Street? But he can't be, we just came from there!'

'We just came from 221B of the twenty-first century. But the letters we received kindly pointed out that we would find him *in our own time*. The address given was clearly a Victorian one.'

'How can you be so sure?'

'It said NW. That was the original postcode of the upper end of the street, when the system was first introduced. The street crossed Marylebone Road, and went on into district W. Today, these districts have been subdivided due to increasing population density, and you will find NW1 and W1 rather than just NW and W on the street signs of Baker Street. Now, we need to find out if they changed the numbering system on the houses as well. Watch out for any empty, old buildings that could have been around the site of Abbey House.'

In former, *present times*, Abbey House had been opposite Mrs Hudson's house. It all seemed quite logical and plausible. So, we made our way down the street, checking house numbers as we went. The street seemed even more menacing in the dark. Especially because we could only hope *not* to see any further proof of our going mad. The blackened bricks of the houses threatened to fall out at us any moment.

Holmes kept quietly mumbling under his breath – he always had a complaint of correction about historical inaccuracies on the tip of his tongue but was stifled by correctness in the last second.

As we walked, we realised that the numbers at the crossing of Marylebone Road weren't anywhere near 200 and they went down as we went further southward. So, after a while, we hurried back up Baker Street, homewards as we thought, but we were in for yet another shock.

There were no houses.

There was no 221.

Only as we walked further up, as far as number 239 would have been in Sherlock's estimate, there slowly appeared behind thick fog the familiar façade of our home. When the fog lifted, we could see No. 219-229 opposite. It seemed weirdly out of its time; Sherlock finally got to issue some of his inaccuracy complaints. A minute later, in which he had also assessed the logistics of the place, we crossed the street and attempted to enter. The door did not move. Sherlock examined the lock, but after a moment scratched his head in disbelief.

'It's open. And no sign of it being jammed in any way. I'm already wearing the damn coat, what else do they want from me?'

It took me a second to remember.

'There was a hat next to the coat on the rack. It looked similar to the one Moran was wearing when you first met me.'

Holmes pursed his lips. 'And why on earth would I be wearing such a ridiculous head garment? Even if I did, it was designed for hunting in Victorian times, not a walk through the city. There is no reason I should—'

'Sherlock! It was there. Just wear it. I'm wearing a turban with a feather, for goodness' sake.'

Holmes raised his eyebrows and came back wearing his deerstalker like in the illustrations. When he stopped next to me, a cold air overcame his face. It seemed like he was unable to move any further. Helplessness spread in his eyes. I kissed his temple. He blinked. Fog rolled up around us and without any further hindrance we entered the building.

* * *

𝕳e will take her from you! 𝕯id you ever doubt that?
𝕳e is not your friend! 𝕳e needs you because you are useful to him. 𝕿hat is not friendship.
𝕳e will take her, and you will suffer again! 𝕭ut 𝕴 can stop him!
𝖄ou can! 𝕴 will rewrite! 𝖄ou will choose the storyline and he will not be in the way any longer. 𝖄ou will finally receive what you deserve, we deserve!
𝕳onour, praise, and the woman you loved the moment she entered the room. 𝕯o you remember?

Distinguishing between the voice in my head and my own had become increasingly difficult during the following weeks, or what seemed like it. It was hard to estimate time under the circumstances. I didn't believe in supernatural occurrences, but I scarcely could explain what exactly happened to me during that time. Whether I could have exorcised the voice, stopped it taking over, or if it was mine all along.

He will take her, and you will suffer! But I can stop him! You can! I will rewrite! I will rewrite!

I was turned into a living echo. Not only my mouth; all my muscles echoed an impulse I could not trace.

You will kill him! I will make you kill him!

A door opened. My rage increased. I had to break free from this! I had to escape this possession! I had to... **kill him!**
My hands tore apart the rope.
I was meant to break loose *now*...

* * *

The house we found ourselves in was strangely labyrinthine. I constantly felt Anne's presence behind my back but tried to stay focussed at all costs. We walked up a narrow iron spiral staircase, then turned right into a long corridor – another spiral staircase – and soon my mind coiled up entirely as we turned left,
        turned right,
turned left,
                turned left again,
        then right,
then left again…

Holmes was cautiously tiptoeing through the building in front of me, until...

The tiniest of noises seemed to shatter time right before my eyes. He *had* been tiptoeing in front of me...

A second ago, surely...

Where am I?

My vision broke into fragments, and I found myself in a house of mirrors. I was everywhere. And suddenly, fragments tumbled into place.

I had lost Sherlock long before this,

long before I had even known...

him.

* * *

When I entered the corridor – or whatever it was that had taken my shape – my eyes were blinded by a tiny crack in the shutters. A gas lamp was flickering outside, and barely anything was visible, but any change in the endless darkness was a different universe to me.

𝕴𝖘 𝖎𝖙 𝖍𝖎𝖘 𝖗𝖎𝖌𝖍𝖙 𝖙𝖔 𝖙𝖆𝖐𝖊 𝖞𝖔𝖚𝖗 𝖑𝖎𝖋𝖊 𝖆𝖓𝖉 𝖒𝖆𝖐𝖊 𝖞𝖔𝖚 𝖆𝖓 𝖊𝖙𝖊𝖗𝖓𝖆𝖑 𝖈𝖔𝖒𝖕𝖆𝖓𝖎𝖔𝖓? 𝕳𝖎𝖘 𝖎𝖓𝖋𝖊𝖗𝖎𝖔𝖗 𝖎𝖓 𝖊𝖛𝖊𝖗𝖞𝖙𝖍𝖎𝖓𝖌? 𝕬 𝖇𝖚𝖒𝖇𝖑𝖎𝖓𝖌 𝖋𝖔𝖔𝖑 𝖙𝖔 𝖊𝖛𝖊𝖗𝖞𝖔𝖓𝖊 𝖞𝖔𝖚 𝖒𝖊𝖊𝖙? 𝕺𝖕𝖊𝖓 𝖞𝖔𝖚𝖗 𝖊𝖞𝖊𝖘! 𝕭𝖊 𝖙𝖍𝖊 𝖕𝖗𝖔𝖙𝖆𝖌𝖔𝖓𝖎𝖘𝖙, 𝖋𝖔𝖗 𝖔𝖓𝖈𝖊, 𝖇𝖊 𝖙𝖍𝖊 𝖕𝖗𝖔𝖙𝖆𝖌𝖔𝖓𝖎𝖘𝖙!

I stumbled forward. It felt like I had lost all my muscles and gained superhuman strength at the same time. I moved like the wind. My perception heightened as it had been through continuous lack of stimulation. I could hear every creak of every board and beam in the entire house.

I had to find Holmes. Someone had to drive the voice out of my head, or it would take over, slowly but surely. Imagining the consequences with horror, I absent-mindedly reached for my belt. There it was. Of course, it was. I never left the house without it. *I am a soldier.*
I killed people.
The fusilier fights for queen and country.
The fusilier is faster.

* * *

She had caught me. I was waiting for paralysis to lock my limbs down, but Anne never showed her face. Instead, she walked behind me as my shadow and laughed when I turned around.

Hundreds and hundreds of turns left me breathless, dizzy in a state of nervous twitching. I could not catch a glimpse of her, only feel her cold hands, hear her rattling, throaty giggles. At the same time, I knew her to have no voice, no breath, but she freely took mine as if it belonged to her.

I tried to run away from her, find Sherlock, find John, *or some way out!*

But there!

At the end of the corridor, she was waiting for me. And this time she wasn't a shadow.

It was her. Shamelessly grinning at me.

The mirrors turned into a kaleidoscope.

I squinted.

'Lily?'

* * *

𝔜ou know those steps. 𝔜ou would recognise them anywhere. And he thinks he is being clever. 𝔥e will pay.

He will hear me! Will this finally stop?
Downstairs, I only need to get downstairs!
A few minutes longer, just a few minutes longer, until I get my life back!
                    𝔍 will have my life back!
Why hasn't he noticed me?
Why can't you see me?

                    𝔜ou are nothing to him.

My grip was firm. My resolution firmer. *Sherlock!* Run!
                                        'Sherlock! *Run!*'

I took aim.
                    𝔗he world will remember me!

Chapter 4

'Mary!'

My life began to recoil.

The queen and the mistress. The two Boleyn girls finally face to face.

This is what Sherlock must have felt like when he discovered he is only a character in a story. My sister Lily was standing at the end of the corridor. She was alive. *Lily* – Anne who was not content with being the mere mistress her sister Mary had been. Anne, the proud Queen of England for only three years. And I was the mere mistress that I had always been.

The house of mirrors burst and left me seeing her clearly.

'Before you kill me,' she began, 'you cannot save me. You never could. It was too late for me before you arrived in Bolivia.'

I knew what she meant. I didn't believe her. I should have. All those years ago. And I didn't believe her even in that moment.

'Mary,' she warmly said. 'I had the life I chose. And I have avenged it.'

'You killed all those people? Here in London?' were the first words I exchanged with my sister in my new life.

'I had to, Mary. They had it coming anyway.' She smiled in her unforgettable, entrancing way that no one could resist. 'You should be able to arrest Eamonn now. Killing him would have been more than he deserves, but I made sure I weakened The Circle enough for you and your detective duo to get to him. I felt they needed some help with that. Fancy *you* hooking up with *that* lot. But then you have always been a connoisseur of crime like me. I can't blame you.' She smiled again.

I was speechless for a moment. There she was, right in front of me, not changed a bit. My perfect copy as ever she had always been.

'Lily, I…'

'Don't worry, my darling princess. You're free now. My work is done. I will go and turn myself in. I can hear them coming now. In return, I only ask one thing.'

I cocked my head to see her from a different angle.

'Know my guilt. It is not yours.'

And with that, she vanished.

* * *

Sherlock ran, I missed. But the fusilier is fast.

𝔦𝔣 in 100 years 𝔦 am only known as the man who invented 𝔖herlock 𝔥olmes, then 𝔦 will have considered my life a failure.

I would catch up with him. *He may be the great detective, but I am a better shot. And he knows.* He darted through the door ahead. I caught up. I kicked the door.

𝔦 am a soldier. 𝔦 kill people.

I didn't need to aim. I needed to miss.

* * *

I remember only the echo of reality splintering again. The shot rang through the entire house and made the floors quaver. My senses were suspended.

* * *

My hypnosis snapped at the sound. How ironic I had never believed in that sort of thing...

I could barely articulate the shock that struck me when I could finally move and see.

There she was on the floor, blood seeping through her clothes, and with it my perception seeping through into my brain. Her fiery hair was spread out around her head like a crown, too heavy for her head. She twitched in pain. This woman that I had loved for so long and had not known.

Sherlock had spun around when I fired, but would have been hit had I not aimed a little to the left. I had done it, I had overcome the voice, but at what cost...

We both were trapped in slow motion. I couldn't remember any of my actions up to the shot, but seeing the gun in my hand and Scarlett lying on the floor was enough even for my deductive abilities. As if I was moving through solid matter, I strained to toss aside my gun and run towards her. Sherlock made one step and not one more when I reached her.

I knelt down and cradled her.

She was smiling at me as if she hadn't seen me in years.

'John!'

I was overwhelmed. Automatically, I pressed my hand on the wound in her chest, but I couldn't tear my eyes away from her face. It had a shadow of sudden aging across it that I did not recognise.

'John, do you remember me?'

I was utterly dumbfounded, but nodded.

'I remember *you*, John. You were so good to me. Despite what you did in the end. You deserve better than me.' She choked and coughed.

'You remember me?' I could only repeat.

She nodded.

My silent tear was lost in the dust. 'I'm so sorry, Scarlett,' was all I could say.

She was still smiling. 'It's not your fault. I had it coming. I'm not in the stories...'

A lightning bolt shot through me, and the air solidified. Her head was dangling off my arm.

Behind me, I could hear a forced breath and a swallowed scream. The air released me, and my head spun round to see Sherlock shaking and clinging to the crumbling wall.

'She's not with you, in the final problem,' he exhaled. 'I should have known...'

I could only shake my head uncomprehendingly.

As he came closer, I clang onto her.

'Don't touch her. Don't you *dare* take this as a case!'

He had come close enough, though. 'John, something's wrong.'

'Stop it! I killed her! The case is closed!' I roared at him.

'Listen to me!' he roared back. 'This is a different dress. It's a similar one, but not the same as she was wearing earlier.'

'What does it matter?! She's *dead!*' I cried; her lifeless neck bent over my arm.

But Sherlock kept on muttering under his breath, walking around searching. *For clues! At this very moment!*

Had I not tossed the gun away, the voice could have very much followed through with what it wanted now.

Finally, I turned back to Scarlett and looked her in the eye. With a shaking hand, I tried to hold her head for her, but her eyes had frozen and her neck was stiff.

'John!' I heard her voice, *one last time*, I thought, and smiled. I didn't care whether I was deceiving myself.

I can hear her.

I was wrong. I had been wrong about everything.

I had not heard Sherlock opening the door and vanishing. I had not heard him open it when he came back. And I had to look twice when I saw Scarlett standing next to him as I turned around.

The body in my arms was weighing down on me, reminding me that *I must be hallucinating!*

Yet, there she was, and she had a different shadow on her face. I knew this shadow.

Suddenly, the woman in my arms felt like a stranger to me. *Am I being hypnotised again? Is this all some hypnotic imagination? Can I make it one?*

Of course, I couldn't. It took me a long time to accept reality, or the shreds of it I had left us with.

* * *

Words would not be spoken when they could not contain the meaning they were given. Words would not be written when they could not tell. The rest was silence.

Many hours later, we had carried the burden of silence home.

Lily Scarlett Vendalle was buried where no one will find her. Anne's head had rolled, and Mary had survived. I knew the story now, my visions stopped. But the guilt persisted.

John was in fragments. I was in pieces. Only Sherlock appeared half torn, held together by secrets he had to keep.

For days, we barely spoke. Only Sherlock told me what he had deduced about John's absence, the substance he had found in his blood, the hypnosis he suspected, remote instructions through a tiny earpiece that he couldn't find.

John knew he could not have a better defendant, but all this time he didn't say a word. Fortunately though, the police struggled to find our Victorian address like we had done. We were on our own.

Mrs Hudson shared the silence.

Ages later, John motioned to Sherlock to speak, still alienated by my presence. The detective gave us the accounts. All he had deduced.

Gradually, I remembered it all.

'I'm afraid, she has been lying to you, us, everyone, involuntarily,' Sherlock began. 'Her name is not Lily Scarlett Vendalle. That is the name of her sister.'

I could not but share Sherlock's bitter smile.

'I have been outwitted by the cliché,' he confessed. 'It was too contrived, too commonplace a twist, and yet too unlikely for me to see it. Highly improbable in real life, but present in a myriad of fictional mysteries. It was too disappointing a solution. Too old a trick. And yet, I have been baffled by nothing but a bad story. Scarlett was her younger twin.'

I was surprised to find my throat capable of uttering sounds, but when John caught my eye, I spoke.

'My name… is Mary Morstan.' My voice was rusty; every word scratched my throat like steel wool. 'We grew up separately from each other. Our parents never told us the reason.'

Here Sherlock took over. 'Scarlett grew up in London with their mother, whose name she carried. Mary stayed behind in India with her father. It appears *Scarlett* was exceptional at school, and eventually went to study at Bart's – with you, John.'

His sigh was quiet, but I could hear his agony as if he had screamed it at me.

After a while, he pulled himself together and asked, 'Are you telling me I never met you before you arrived here without your memory?'

I nodded and gulped.

'Are you telling me, you never were the person I thought you were, and I couldn't see?'

His voice was bitterly calm.

'You did see, John. Remember how often you said I was now a different person?' I tried carefully.

It wasn't enough for him.

'*You* never *were* going to remember me. Because there is nothing to remember? Is this what you're telling me? I took in a total stranger and fell for her... trick?'

I was shaking with guilt.

'I swear it wasn't a trick, John. I beg you, think it anything but that,' I croaked with the little firmness I had left.

With a grim expression, John turned back to Sherlock. 'When did you know?'

'Too late,' the detective replied, his voice at its lowest pitch.

A few minutes' silence. John was contemplating throwing Sherlock against the wall, I could see it in his eyes. He seemed, however, to have decided to hear the story first.

Sherlock continued, 'Scarlett joined The Red Circle as a smuggler while still at university. I don't know how or where she got them, but somehow, she managed to acquire the M and B Boleyn necklaces. With her connections, it was worth a fortune, but also wouldn't stay a secret for very long. Soon, it attracted the attention of Eamonn Doyle, who has been sending us his kind regards in threads. His connection to *The Strand Magazine* stories is still not quite clear to me. However, I can say he was one of the more powerful members of The Red Circle, and he proposed to make a fortune establishing a smugglers' network in South America. She agreed, and that was the last you saw of her until a few days ago.'

John's indignation could have ignited the entire room.

As a reflex, I tried to touch his hand, but he pulled it away.

'In Bolivia, she specialised in becoming an assassin, and committed the twenty-three murders catalogued in her file. I knew Mary could not have done it, because all her accounts, all her memories were never of the killing, only ever of the weapon in her hand and the body in front of her. These killings were murders, meticulously planned and coldly executed. They were not part of her trauma. She was innocent, and began realising someone was trying to frame her. It seemed only too likely that it was the same person who committed the murders. But since Mary seemed to have been covering up Lily's tracks voluntarily, it was implausible after all. The more probable solution was that a member of the organisation was trying to use the situation of the escaped twin to their advantage. That's why I didn't want Mary to see the file under any circumstance. It is possible to alter someone's long-term memory with the easiest of tricks. A faked photograph will do. Unfortunately, The Circle took care to jog her memory just the right amount; it didn't take long for her to be more and more convinced she had committed the crimes. This does not happen so easily when the actual memory is less painful than the imagined one. The only possible explanation was that she had been trying to protect someone and would rather take on the guilt herself than failing to save them.'

'Scarlett,' I threw in carefully, 'had contacted me when I moved to study in the UK. We met up and liked each other actually. I think she knew she was getting herself into trouble and needed someone to be there if she needed help. She had fallen in love with Eamonn and could sense that she wasn't breaking free from it unless she asked for help. Sisters are good for that. Sisters are also good for confessions. She confided in me that she had the two famous necklaces. She meant to give them to me one day when she had found a person with enough skill to produce a fake for her to sell. Of course, she never did. Until I arrived here.'

Sherlock gave me a moment to recover, then explained, 'Her brain twisted this into a protecting mechanism. Scarlett did ask for help and your lives intertwined much like the story of the Boleyn sisters.'

'He betrayed her. Got bored with her, took to other women and arranged for the police to get rid of her,' I said. 'When she called me, it was as if she had awoken from hypnosis. She resented her old life and wanted to start again. I wanted her to have a second chance – she was my sister, and I felt responsible to do anything in my power. I had seen goodness in her and believed her that she had genuinely changed. Her plan was simple–'

'She had arranged,' Sherlock interrupted, 'for you to take her place in the organisation while she dismantled them by giving evidence to the authorities and assembling a big enough police force to do all the necessary arrests.'

It was John's turn to interject. 'Why all the twin shuffling? Surely, she must be found out easily, when' – he gulped – 'Scarlett could have just figured out a better escape plan and handed in the evidence herself? Or why not give' – he gulped again – 'Mary…' – he shook his head – 'the evidence for her to hand in?'

'Escaping from such a brilliantly structured organisation as The Red Circle is almost impossible, especially when police are hard to reach. And Mary could not speak Spanish or an official local language, meaning in delivering the evidence, she would be unable to explain her own innocence or role in this state of affairs.

'In any case, they went through with Scarlett's plan, and Mary took her place. They swapped at an opportune moment, Scarlett having informed her sister of all there had been between her and Eamonn Doyle, and all there was to know about the organisation. Mary had two tasks: covering up the evidence against Scarlett on the latest of her jobs, so she would not go to prison, and preventing The Circle from finding out that Scarlett had left for the police. Mary played her part well.'

'How would you know that?' The bittersweet memories of that time stinging in my chest.

'You grew so close to Eamonn Doyle that you ended up with a serious head injury,' Sherlock pointed towards the scar at my temple, 'and no memory, but escaped with your life.' He raised his eyebrow. 'Revenge suggests itself just as much as some form of attachment.'

'I didn't play my part,' I confessed. 'He saw that I wasn't as weary as Scarlett and had some inspiration left. I was useful to him in pointing out loopholes in his plans, in a way that Scarlett hadn't been, because I have always been good at predicting what people might think. He must have felt his relationship rekindle, and it made me feel quite alive to be deceiving him so brazenly.

'At the same time, I knew if he found out I was a different person, he would admire me for the skill of my deception rather than shoot me on the spot. And I was right. Only, he wasn't going to let Scarlett go as easily. I was covering for her, but she was betraying The Circle. You will understand that the latter was unforgivable. And while I may have not been guilty of my sister's crimes, I was guilty of not preventing them. After a month with Eamonn, I would not have betrayed him to the police. I was glad to keep Scarlett out of prison, and I did not care what happened to The Circle. But I would not let them arrest Eamonn, no matter the cost. So, the night when they came for him, I betrayed my sister to save him.

'The usual team of four, Achmet James and Jenny Vandeleur, Eamonn and I – posing as Scarlett – were on a job to recover a vast amount of drugs from a "secret" hideout which another gang had "seemingly" been forced to abandon that day, and Scarlett had incited an ambush just there. Achmet had suspected me for a while. He threatened to kill me after I had sent Eamonn over to the other side of the cave under false pretences. It was then that the first shot was fired, killing him on the spot. When Eamonn came back to see what was wrong, excuses could not keep him away any longer. I had to tell him that someone had tipped off the police. At that point, I thought Scarlett was well out of danger, but I was wrong. She was with the police when they came. It was a massacre.'

As my voice trailed away, Sherlock took over again, his face seemingly illuminating at every turn he saw the story take.

'You thought she was killed that night, didn't you? It wasn't just survivor's guilt. Your vision of her being executed – you saw someone shoot her, and it wasn't just anyone, but Eamonn Doyle. The perfect parallel to the Tudor story. The lover executes the beloved. Of course, she wasn't beheaded, but you were beginning to suffer a trauma that lost you your mind for quite a while. The massacre opened your eyes for a brief moment, but then your brain tried to conceal everything in pain and shock. My guess is, you escaped barely wounded after passing out and everyone thinking you dead. The police officers were all killed, with The Circle recoiling back underground.

'When you woke up, you probably found your sister, only unconscious like you, but thought her dead, and as you had no time to lose before they noticed your body was missing. So, you ran for it. In your state, it must have felt like weeks in the desert, which is why that flight was still so prevalent in your visions. If you felt, deep down, that your sister might still be alive, you also felt responsible for her death by abandoning her. Being heavily wounded and within the reach of The Red Circle, she would have no chance of surviving. Eamonn would make sure of that. Am I correct?'

I nodded, a lump forming in my throat. My grief suddenly hit me as I recalled the feeling of seeing her alive earlier, of being relieved, only to be struck by the same pain moments later. It was still my fault my sister was dead.

Sherlock looked at me understandingly. 'We can stop here for now.'

But I shook my head. 'Eamonn caught up with me. Of course, he did. He knew me too well. He found me and tortured me, twisted my mind into believing myself guilty of Scarlett's crimes, her death and his "inconvenience." It was no good that I screamed that I had been loyal to him. He kept forcing words down my throat until I couldn't tell what was real and what wasn't. My scoliosis must have come from the way he twisted me. I think he could see the hallucinations in my eyes and knew he only had to keep tipping me back into them for his revenge to work.

'"You want to go to the police," he kept saying, "it's your own sentence you will receive." The last thing I remember before I woke up here is his grim smile as he dashed out my memory with a bare stone. The edges dug so deep into my head—' I stopped abruptly.

A long silence followed.

John seemed to freeze at the description of my pain, while Sherlock seemed to be fascinated by my survival. I could feel him reading me more than he had ever done.

'You were drugged whenever you woke up,' Sherlock added after a while. 'Knowing your sister had lived in the UK before coming to Bolivia, they brought you back here. Correct me if my deductions are wrong, but as I see it, this is what happened: it was not until Scarlett had also escaped and made it to a hospital that they knew she was alive – otherwise they would have easily stopped her with her injuries – but she made it to the UK. Later Eamonn decided to use that to his own advantage.

'Now and then, when you were in the hospital, someone from The Circle came to visit you, took you outside while you were sleepwalking, drugged to think you were dreaming; all this to train your body, as well as your abilities to shoot. That way, my own deductions would be able to identify you as an assassin. Through Moriarty's web, they were put in touch with him and offered to plant the most destructive case to any detective nemesis of his heart's desire, for a high fee. I could flatter myself thinking that is why he picked me, but John's connection to Scarlett simply made the choice irresistible. They were clever enough to know that nothing would lead to John or me handing you over to the police, which would make us suspects in the eyes of the authorities.

'They also knew how to further your visions, and that we would try to find out where they came from. While you were with us, they kept planting retrieval cues where you would see them unexpectedly, so your visions kept coming back to blur your feeling of actual memory and hallucination. That way, they could ensure that you gradually retrieved just enough information to believe yourself guilty but unable to betray The Circle in any believable way. They expected a confession from a guilty heart, which unquestionably the innocent woman must feel to be the right thing to do.

'Then suddenly, Scarlett came back into the story. About her motives, I can only speculate, but my guess is that she found out what Eamonn had done to you, and where they had brought you. Then, meticulously, she traced back the agents who were working "Mary's case." She didn't know that they were meant to keep you alive for a confession, and she didn't need to know what they were doing to you. You having helped her to break out, she tried to do the same for you. So, she killed every one of Eamonn's agents she could find who came close to you. She was a brilliant assassin, I must say. The first one she killed was at Gower Mews where we first found out about the involvement about The Circle. However, Eamonn realised what was happening, had the agent shot on the doorstep before he could tell us anything and developed an even more cunning plan to convict you.

'As the killings increased, he abducted you and altered his own file to help us find the bodies in time for certain fresh evidence to lead the police to you. Of course, he knew that Scarlett was a professional, so she would leave no fingerprints and any evidence distinguishing her from Mary would be hidden. Instead, there was likely going to be some DNA that Scarlett would leave at the crime scene, and he could trust the police to find it. If there wasn't any, he could easily supply it from you yourself when he was torturing you. And all that time his methods were so subtle, they would certainly escape the notice of the police, and even if I had told them I suspected him to be planting the evidence there – having discarded the twin theory from the get go – they would not believe me.

'Discrediting me was his second objective in all this. Because not only did he alter his file to make us find her faster; you will remember the agents were all killed in a location where we had previously solved a murder, pointing the police towards us, and us towards Mary, to make us question our trust in her. Moriarty's criminal consulting, clearly. The only link I could not find out was how they knew where and in exactly what order we solved our cases. I suppose they must have read *The Strand Magazine*,' Sherlock tried to joke.

'Is that why you think they're working with Moriarty?' John asked with no expression.

'It was Eamonn's messages that first led us to them, so why not?' I added.

'See, I don't think it was him actually putting those messages here,' Sherlock objected. 'No sign of a forced entry any time a message appeared, you see. But it is possible that he and Moriarty connected their plans—'

Here John got some sign of life back. 'No sign of a forced entry!? What are you implying? That Mrs Hudson put them there!? Or Sca- Mary under hypnosis? Just admit you couldn't find anything – this is absurd enough as it is!'

Sherlock didn't say anything, but I felt it was not because he agreed, but because he couldn't yet prove the theory he had. And if I wasn't mistaken, a theory was forming behind his eyes that very second.

Is it something John said?

My head was weary, and I couldn't use it quite the way I wanted to. I could barely stand where I was near the door, throughout the conversation, ready to leave when someone asked me to.

Of course, I was blaming myself for everything. Feeling John's heart slowly disintegrating at the realisation of who I was and what we had done, under the weight of our false attachment crumbling in its foundations, I had forfeited all hope of rebuilding his trust. I was a lost case. Once again, I found myself at the end of a lifetime. Or so I thought…

Up to this point, I had felt paralysed and numb. All I could bring myself to wish was for John to know the truth. Now that he did, I felt my heart disintegrate as well.

Chapter 5

My brain had tried to shut down the turmoil caused by the turn of events, turning out different, turning against me, turning my mind upside down. I could not bring myself to wish that Mary was still in love with me. I had killed her sister, the very person she had risked her life for, the very person I had loved more than any woman in my life.

I did not know whether I could ever believe Sherlock his deductions about my drug-induced hypnosis. The voice in my head was too similar to my own. I knew I had only shot to miss Sherlock, but I also knew how easy it was for me to pull a trigger. Hadn't a part of me been conscious when I killed her? The part of me that was the monster I had told Mary I had learnt to live with, back when she had first moved in? The soldier had executed his orders. I deeply detested that part of me for it, but I was unable to escape the role, as discipline seemed the only way out for myself when I had been left a shell of my hopes, prisoner of my actions, a victim of an increasingly uncontrollable mind. In hindsight, I can see that this was what both Sherlock and Mary had been going through then, but at the time I did not have the strength to understand.

Of course, I could not tell Sherlock and Mary that I had been hearing the voice of the abhorrent author who claimed to have invented us. In time, I naturally doubted that memory, that thought in itself, and wondered if it hadn't been my fault entirely. The only thing I could remember to my own advantage had been my trying to warn Sherlock even under hypnosis, and the fact that the shot I had fired would have missed him hadn't Scarlett appeared just there just then... Or had I subconsciously meant to kill her? More than once, I tried to turn myself in to the police, but New Scotland Yard had vanished. Despite my inability to defend my actions, both Sherlock and Mary, and consequently Mrs Hudson, were treating me as if I was entirely innocent.

I did not feel entitled to their kindness, nor did I feel entitled to any form of relationship with Mary. It was foolish to disregard the months we had spent together, the feelings we had had for each other. It was also foolish to think they would be undermined be the false assumptions we had had about each other. But I just wished I could forget; all the memories felt like surgery without narcotics.

After a while, there were a few moments when I felt strong, more forgiving. I tried to figure out who could have mentally manipulated me into killing someone by posing as the voice of a most likely non-existent writer who claimed to have control over my life. But it was also in those moments that I began listening to the voice again.

I had happened not to listen when Mary must have told us what Mycroft had found out about Dr Conan Doyle. Sherlock, on the other hand, seemed to have found something even more alarming to himself than any of the previous events. He did not show it, but I could see it, even through the dead eyes of my soldier shell.

It was the fear of death in his face that slowly allowed me to break free and take my voice back.

* * *

It was a Wednesday when John finally spoke. Hearing his voice in a manner that seemed almost normal healed a great many of the wounds from the last two weeks. There was hope.

'Sherlock, I've... found something,' I heard him say through the kitchen door. Of course, I was *not* listening in on a private conversation without the consent of either party, and *neither* was Mrs Hudson who, *of course*, had just *incidentally* happened to pass by and decided to position a chair next to me quietly. We both smiled at each other.

'And what's that?' Sherlock almost sounded cautious.

For a second, we thought we had been discovered, but he merely enquired after John's discovery.

'I've seen the magazine. 1893, December issue.'

We heard some clattering as Sherlock apparently clutched the table edge.

After a moment, he seemed to have recovered and said rather steadily, 'I can see you haven't read it.'

'That's a shot in the dark, you can't tell me you've deduced that.'

'It was a shot in the dark. A good one though. And I would be able to deduce it, if I were to go and check the magazine now. I memorise its position in the drawer every time I put it back and I am absolutely certain I could find your fingerprints on it, but not in it.'

John chuckled, slightly irritated, but not disapprovingly. Mrs Hudson and I beamed at each other. For the moment, we didn't care one ounce about what was threatening Sherlock – it was like soothing balm on our souls to hear them heal back together.

'Why didn't you read it?' Sherlock asked with his warmest voice.

'Because I know what's in it. Did you think I wouldn't recognise that look on your face? I know you, and I know that look,' John explained, his voice almost as warm, but slightly worried.

Sherlock was silent for a moment. 'I will find whoever was responsible for your hypnosis,' he slowly, carefully insisted.

'You know it wasn't as simple as that. Sherlock, don't follow the story. Whatever it says, whatever you do or don't do, *leave it be*. Slip between the lines, skip the page, I don't know. Just promise me, you'll fight.'

'You can rely on that, Watson.'

Mrs Hudson and I exchanged a glance, raising our eyebrows.

'What?' John pretended he hadn't heard.

'Did I say something?' Sherlock asked innocently.

'Oh, never mind. Just don't keep secrets from me. I know I'm an idiot in your mind, but I can help. And you would be an idiot if you didn't accept it.'

'I would like to return the compliment,' Sherlock retorted, half amused, half serious.

'No, I mean it, Sherlock. I found something else.'

'What have you found?'

'Thread, in Mrs Hudson's kitchen.'

'You don't mean...' Sherlock started.

So did Mrs Hudson next to me.

'Yes,' John said. 'Red, and crinkled in zigzags, just like from your buttonhole. There wasn't much of it left, but I'm sure you'll be able to find fibres of it on her iron.'

'Well, we'd better go and ask her about it then, shall we?'

Our landlady nearly fell off her chair as Sherlock opened the door.

'I have long suspected your husband wasn't the only family member that needed bringing to justice,' he announced in a pretend-supercilious manner. 'Who is it this time?'

Part 9: Napoleon's Grave

Chapter 1

'My son,' said Mrs Hudson, our housekeeper. Mrs Hudson, our friend. Mrs Hudson, the woman with the sleepy tea. Mrs Hudson, the woman with the drugged biscuits. Mrs Hudson, the dancer with an executed husband and a murdered brother.

'Not your housekeeper!' I could hear her say now. 'The rest... is pretty much accurate.'

Sherlock raised an eyebrow. 'Did he crash your car?'

'Don't be silly, dear. He arranged the killing of a few people, I stopped counting at around 70 – not at all involuntarily – and he is currently planning to kill you. I take it, you're not surprised by this, but I assume you're surprised at my admitting it.' The old lady smirked.

The Great Detective was indeed baffled, and I could say no less of the rest of us.

'Seeing as you have been working for him for some time, I cannot but conclude from your behaviour,' Sherlock reasoned after a moment, 'that you intended for us to find you out.' He raised his other eyebrow as well.

'Well, I promised not to betray him to you, so you had to find out by yourselves. It's not my fault it took you so long. But you were rather enjoying my *herbal soothers*, weren't you, Sherlock?'

I pulled a face.

'Where did you think they came from?' Mary enquired with equally raised eyebrows.

'I–'

'—thought they just sort of happened?'

Sherlock gulped.

Mrs Hudson smiled. 'It takes an addict to know one, John. How do you think we met?'

'I was on a case, I tell you,' Sherlock mumbled through clenched teeth.

'Oh, I know you were, dear, but you were enjoying it to the last drop.'

By this time, I was boiling inside, as anyone with a pinch of common sense would be, but evidently Sherlock only possessed every other kind of sense.

'Who is that ominous son of yours then? Eamonn Doyle?' I asked our landlady.

'Oh, no. Little Jimmy... Well, he always had a tendency to be dramatic, not unlike some other people I must say.' She gave Sherlock an ironic look.

'Oh God, the messages weren't from Eamonn, were they?' Mary realised.

Mrs Hudson slyly shook her head.

'But who could they have been from? Who wanted to help Mary remember and tell us about the stories in the magazine? Mary isn't even in them!' I blustered.

'I wouldn't hold out too much hope that Mary Morstan is not one of the characters in our stories, but then who am I to be pessimistic?' Sherlock forced a smile.

'What if Conan Doyle decided to get rid of her?' I thought out loud. *Would that give her freedom, or take her away from us?*

'I can watch out perfectly well for myself, thank you,' Mary interrupted. 'Presuming the messages were from him. But who is Little Jimmy?'

'You don't mean—'

'James Moriarty, yes,' Mrs Hudson confirmed coolly.

My eyes nearly popped out.

'Or at least he calls himself that, because it means "the art of dying" in Latin,' she added, unimpressed by my amazement. 'I expect our relation will have been discarded in the account of this story in the magazine.'

We all knew she meant the story Sherlock had found most recently.

'So, Moriarty is in that story?' Mary surmised.

'Yes,' he replied briskly.

'Did you think he also just sort of happened?' Mrs Hudson asked with the stern look of a cross mother.

'That's what he does in the story.'

'Bad storytelling. Little Jim deserved better. I've never seen a more magnificent criminal mind. I am sure you share the sentiment, Sherlock. That doesn't mean I agree with his inclinations; I got out of the whole business long ago. Have you ever wondered why I offered you affordable rent in Central London? When you saved me from being convicted for murdering my brother, I knew my son was interested in you. Not least because he had helped my husband with the murder. But you never made the connection. If you didn't see his relation to me, it's because you weren't looking.

'In any case, 221B was supposed to cover your tracks for a while. And Jim knows how well I can handle a gun. So, no, I am not just your landlady; I am your watchdog.' Mrs Hudson proudly folded her arms.

'And what made you abandon that role?' Sherlock enquired with a sudden coldness in his voice.

'You're getting it wrong; the messages weren't *all* from Little Jim - although, he very much let the others happen, because they suited him,' Mrs Hudson defended herself, but I couldn't stop feeling slightly uneasy about the quiver in her voice. 'The messages were signed with ED, but again, you missed something. ED in Morse without the space—'

'Is L!' Mary suddenly exclaimed. 'Remember when you found that tattoo on Barker? Are you saying my sister was responsible for some of the messages?'

Mrs Hudson nodded slowly. 'The ones about you, yes. I met her when I killed Barker.'

Here, our landlady smirked as we gasped, then continued: 'He had intelligence about Little Jim that he wanted out of the way. He gave me no chance to refuse. Barker was carrying a tracker which Lily had hacked, and she discovered me shooting him. So, in exchange for her silence, I laid out the messages in the flat for her. From all I could see, your sister was trying to help you, although God knows what you got yourself into. I knew I couldn't lose your trust as long as Jim was around, so I decided the innocent role in the background of the stories would suit me for now.'

'It is not our trust you were worried about, Mrs Hudson,' Sherlock simply declared. 'Tell us the whole story.'

Mrs Hudson sighed. 'I'm not pretending not to be on any of the MI5 registers. You had to find out by yourselves, but now that you have, I might as well confess.'

Mary and I could not stop exchanging bewildered glances.

'It appears that Little Jimmy had the goodness to save my husband from execution, which I didn't tell you, because I know how it hurts your pride, but it also meant that my husband was looking to take revenge on the person responsible. Jim knew that that was me, and threatened to tell my husband, should I not play along in his wonderful magic tricks.'

'Simple blackmail then?' I concluded, disappointed in Moriarty's methods for once.

'Of course, blackmail is always simple.' Mrs Hudson pursed her lips. 'And here I was, thinking the great Sherlock Holmes surely would find out within an instant, with all the clues I left lying around. But I couldn't do it too obviously, or my husband would have showed up to finish me off in no time. I have always been happy taking risks, but now I am not quite as capable of wriggling out of them as I used to be.

'I knew my child was a devil from the moment he first drugged me with my own biscuits. But he's my son, so what can I say? I've been dreaming of someone putting him in a nice safe jail cell for decades, and if anyone could do it, it's this madman over here, who's so like Jim, he only has to put himself in his shoes to find and convict him. After my husband was executed, or failed to be, I never heard a word from my son or the rest of my family, until about two years ago, when Jim first showed up in London.

'He had stolen my car. When I found him, he gave me biscuits, apologised and told me he could have me killed very quickly if I didn't honour the family connection and made his favourite detective "dance." So, I thought I'd invite him round to pay his respects and leave a few magazines now and again. Except, I didn't think that at all, until someone suggested it. A very helpful gentleman on the tube with a strange moustache, a round face and a pointy nose. There was something compelling in his voice, and I did as he said.'

'And you have taken care of your husband, I perceive,' Sherlock coolly remarked. 'You used to wear your wedding ring, but not so now, why?'

'Oh yes, stroke of luck. He ambled right into my trap for Barker. Being a member of The Red Circle can be quite useful. The man on the tube put me on to it, actually, I don't know what it was he said. I knew that Barker and my husband were acquainted so it was child's play to let the latter be sent, on Barker's own advice, to of The Circle's murderous exit ritual happening at Gower Mews. Meanwhile, I went after Barker myself. It could have been my idea, really.'

I could not believe none of us had found her out when we examined both Barker and the Red Circle victim at Gower Mews. The worst of it was that I believed the woman. I was petrified. And so was Sherlock. We could hardly believe we hadn't recognised Mr H...

'Thank you, you may go now, Mrs Hudson,' Sherlock suddenly dismissed her. Thick clouds of thought were wrinkling up his brooding forehead.

'Thank you. This has been quite an interrogation. There is no reason to believe I am further entangled in your mess. I am not just a plot device, but the protagonist of my own life whether anyone decides to believe it or not!' She almost sounded like a feminist adaptation of herself. 'I trust you now know what to do,' she addressed Sherlock cryptically.

His eyes narrowed. 'You may depend upon it.'

* * *

I did not look at the story in the latest *Strand* issue. Vendors had now appeared in the streets selling it, all of them dressed in Inverness capes like Sherlock's. With all my might, I started telling myself what inventions we had had in the present, what knowledge we had acquired. After a while, we even got a client who was quite astonished at Sherlock's modern methods. His case was too simple for an illustrated magazine's readership. That was probably why Sherlock took it. The man's name was John Smith and the case he brought was of a stolen police, originally placed in front of his house. Sherlock quickly traced it to Cardiff, arranging for it to be returned by Billy who afterwards enjoyed some tea with us. I couldn't help but wonder why we couldn't do more for him. He could have been an excellent police officer, I thought. Definitely better than the 'Bow Street Runners' or 'Peelers' who were now populating Baker Street, as well as the rest of London.

Fortunately for us though, the lack of training and methods for catching criminals in Victorian times led to none of them detecting us as fugitives of the law.

'So, you want me to find Moran?' Billy enquired, munching on three biscuits at once.

John and I looked at Sherlock with astonishment.

'Surely you can't send the boy into danger like that,' John complained.

'He's not a kid! He's 29, for God's sake,' Sherlock shot back, his mouth full of cake.

'The kid's jus' a disguise to be less suspicious. Especially in Victorian times there are lo's o' homeless kids.'

John groaned. 'Now don't tell me you've done your research...'

'I did, sir! Mos' diligen'ly, sir!' Billy replied in a boyish voice.

'The fact that he fooled you into thinking he was underage should qualify him for the job, don't you think?' Sherlock finished smugly.

John just scowled, while I had to look the other way to conceal a smirk.

'So what's the plan?' I asked.

'Well,' Sherlock began, 'when you first saw Moran, he was wearing a ridiculous deerstalker. I take it, he must have been in on Moriarty's plan to move us back in time. Now, I think he might be in on the big case that is closing in on us too, and I want to know the role he is going to play.'

Soon, Billy had gone and the detective looked more like a statue of himself than like an actual human being. John had gone downstairs to talk to Mrs Hudson. I took the opportunity to corner Sherlock.

'Why aren't you telling us about this big case, Sherlock?'

Sherlock waited a moment, perhaps because he wanted to make sure John was not about to come upstairs, or perhaps because he was contemplating whether I could be trusted. Finally, he replied very slowly, 'You would try to stop me.' His eyes were as close to begging me to stay silent as Sherlock Holmes could ever get to begging.

I made a step towards him. 'Why aren't you telling me?'

'You already know the essentials,' he murmured hoarsely. 'Don't you think I could deduce someone else's deductions?'

'Prove it.'

'You noticed something was wrong when I acted unnecessarily recklessly, and jumped to the conclusion that there was another magazine, because you have seen these stories tamper with my sanity. Except, I refused to talk to you or John about it instead of involving you in the hunt for clues as I had done before. I also faked disinterest in it, clearly unconvincingly, but it worked, because at the time John was missing and you had other things on your mind. Now that the situation has changed, naturally you would start to think about it again, just as John has done. And you would, given my continued secretive behaviour and reserved mood, have to assume the story was still affecting me.'

'You could have been thinking about the mystery of all stories as a whole, surely?'

'I have been doing that ever since the second one appeared, as would only be logical to presume, so you immediately ruled that out. This must be a new threat level. Considering threats in the story, your mind quite correctly now jumped to the conclusion that a new, more important figure than before must have appeared in ink – one James Moriarty. The only match for me.

'That would finally explain why he had Mrs Hudson put the messages here – to lead us to him and his great coup. Now, you've seen me making preparations for an attack coming from Moran, and obviously Moriarty would only involve his best people if there were to be an attempt on my life. You assume further that I see this as an opportunity to finally catch my nemesis, but fear that my life might end in it, and yet I have not at all tried to flee from the story approaching. Given the fact that you have asked me about this particular topic while John is out, I can therefore assume you will not tell anyone about this. I can also deduce, since you know I will not be dissuaded from my course of action, that you are not trying to stop me, but to find out why I am so willingly facing death.'

I gulped, nodding. I *had* hoped he wouldn't go that far, but then he *was* Sherlock Holmes.

Sherlock took his time to reply. First, he smiled bitterly, looking down. Then, he looked up at the ceiling as if to accuse the heavens for bringing this down on him. When he turned back to me, everything but the melancholy premonition of a Hamlet had vanished from his face, and he quietly confessed, with a second smile:

'It's a good story.'

Chapter 2

In the following days, we received a visit from Sadie and Finch who imediatelly huddled in front of the fireplace with steaming cups of hot chocolate. Their clothes had quite deteriorated into Victorian rags, but they insisted they could blend in better that way. Sherlock rightly deduced, however, that they hadn't come to warm themselves up.

'Have you heard from Billy?' he inquired.

"E gave us a lis' o' places 'e was gonna search, a couple o' days ago,' Sadie explained. 'Since then, we 'aven' 'eard from 'im.'

'We 'eard from someone else though,' Finch chimned in. 'We was wonderin' if we coul' be allowed to talk to Mr Mycrof'.'

'*Were* wondering,' Sherlock corrected the poor boy mechanically. 'You tell me what you're talking about and I'll decide if I can bear the inconvenience inherent to my brother's presence.'

'We think we may 'ave found ou' one of Moriar'y's men. 'E's been lurking around Baker Street an' Regen''s Park for two weeks straigh',' Sadie said.

'An' we seen 'im escaping from Mycrof's agen's a few weeks ago, after a bank robbery,' Finch added. 'So, we pu' two an' two together an' though' you migh' wanna se' your brother's men back on 'is trail.'

Sherlock shot me a glance, raising an eyebrow – his let's-go-and-catch-ourselves-a-criminal look. It was that kind of look when directed at *me*, mind. When he raised his eyebrows at other people, on the other hand, it was usually an attempt at concealing his indignation at their stupidity. I gave him my what-are-you-waiting-for smirk and in no time we were off, leaving Mary to take care of Finch and Sadie.

'What are we thinking then?' I asked on the way.

'If this man has been lurking around here for any length of time, it won't be long before Moriarty discovers our location, whether it exists in Victorian times or not. My guess is there will be an attempt made on us at 221B, the only question is when and where will we find a safe place to hide.'

'You're not guessing, Sherlock. You know. I can tell. How?'

Here, the great detective suddenly became ever so slightly insecure about what to say, but he soon caught himself.

'I think that Billy would have been in touch sooner, if the plan hadn't already proceeded. Moran is looking for us as much as we are looking for him, and if he were still planning his steps, Billy could have overheard the whole thing and reported back. As it is, he hasn't dropped a single message, and instead we have a criminal on our heels, who evidently is acting out the plan already.'

'Not sure if it's just me finding that deduction a bit vague, but I digress. Keep your secrets, Sherlock, you always have, and I'm not the one to stop you, however much I would love to.'

For the rest of our short walk to Regent's Park, we were silent. It was dark and slightly foggy – an early winter afternoon. Sherlock greatly resented the squeaking of the metal doorgate, which had only become louder in the past, so – tall as he was – he easily climbed over a hedge. I was left to scramble after him.

The park was almost deserted, which could only be expected on such a cold day. It also meant that sneaking up on someone unseen wasn't going to be very easy. While Sherlock was looking around for clues, I preferred to ask a man leaning against a tree, reading his newspaper, if he had seen anything strange. That might have been the daftest approach of mine so far, but considering Sherlock hadn't paid the man any attention, I felt I could hardly be blamed.

When the man looked up from his newspaper, I was instantly taken aback. I had not anticipated this. I hadn't expected to see his face again ever, but when he stared straight down at me my sense of storytelling reprimanded me for not expecting him back in the plot. The man whose car Scarlett – Mary – had run into all those weeks back in our long-gone present day; the age of sense. The same man Sherlock had identified as Ignatius Thurston, whose file had replaced that of Eamonn Doyle.

'Can I help you?' he asked innocently.

The lack of guilt paralysed me for only one second, but that was enough for me to form the resolution to knock the man out.

'Well done, John,' Sherlock scoffed at me. 'Mycroft would be delighted with your methods of questioning people.'

Thurston had slumped down on my shoulder, so I had to hold up his head for Sherlock to see his face. At this unexpected sight, my friend grinned suavely and repeated, 'Well done, John!' with some actual appreciation.

We used Sherlock's coat as a straitjacket as we carefully snuck back towards the park entrance. At one point, I heard a rattling in a bush, but as no further noises followed, I brushed it off as a squirrel. Needlessly, I started wondering if the grey squirrels had driven the red squirrels out of England in Victorian times already.

Still, we had our man and there was no need to worry now. Until, that was, Thurston started wriggling violently as we tried to open the doorgate to the park. He almost kicked me and I nearly dropped his feet, but Sherlock calmly said, 'Allow me,' and punched the man again. We got to Baker Street without any further trouble and we heaved him up the stairs into the living room. Once we had propped Thurston up on a chair and splashed some water in his face he slowly came to.

'Would you be so kind to tell me where I am?' he asked in a strained tone.

'That's not the man we saw!' Sadie exclaimed, looking up as he spoke.

'No, but *we* saw him; he hit her with a car,' I gestured towards Mary.

'What? I did nothing of the kind,' the man protested. 'I demand to know who you are and where you take the right to detain me from!'

'We're the archenemies of your criminal mastermind boss, and you shut up unless you're answering some questions!'

'John,' Sherlock stopped me. 'I believe we were on the wrong track. This man clearly works for Mycroft. We should tell him to disguise his agents better next time.'

'What do you want?' Thurston hissed through clenched teeth.

'You were on Mary's case, weren't you? You followed her from Bolivia, even helped staging her discovery in London by the police when she lost her memory, am I correct?' Sherlock deduced, raising an eyebrow.

I looked at him like a lion about to tear into his prey.

'Before your tender-hearted companion eats me alive, yes, you are quite correct unfortunately,' Thurston growled.

Sherlock caught my fist in the air with a quick move.

'How can you tell? How, Sherlock?' I hissed at him.

'Easy, he just killed the man Sadie and Finch saw earlier,' Sherlock stated as if he was talking about the weather.

Sadie, Finch, Mary and I all turned towards the detective in astonishment.

Thurston didn't move. That was confession enough to me.

Sherlock proceeded, 'You saw the rat in the bush earlier, John? It was there because Moriarty's man wasn't buried deep enough. Why bury a man in a public park – and more importantly how to do that unseen? Well, it's as convenient a hiding place as any, if you consider that nobody will start digging there. The gardeners would be appalled! So, all he had to do was a bit of landscaping at night, disguising the spot well, but it seems he spotted Sadie and Finch earlier and expected us subsequently, or he would have dug a deeper hole.'

'But how do you know he killed him?'

He gaped me but continued, 'Because he is wearing gloves but no hat, suggesting he is not feeling cold enough to make gloves necessary unless you need to cover your fingertips. Also, the bleached marks of worn-out fabric on the outside of his coat pocket suggest a very small and very cliché pocket gun, which he stuffed away in haste. You can see that there is a tiny black spot on the inside of the fabric here, which must have appeared when the gun, still hot from the friction at the muzzle, burnt the silk. Then there is just a slight hint of earthy dust on the trousers from kneeling down to dig the hole. And why would he kill one of Moriarty's men with so rare a weapon if he wasn't working for the secret service?'

Thurston pursed his lips but didn't contradict Sherlock.

'Except you're not exactly doing your job, are you, Mr Thurston?'

Here the man looked up at Sherlock, almost frightened.

'You hit Mary with your car to protect her from the secret service stationed at The Royal Courts of Justice that day, didn't you? I expect there was a price on her head and you knew how keen the other agents would be to collect it. I don't know your motives, but I believe if we go back to the park now and start digging, we will excavate the remains of Eamonn Doyle – or whatever the rat has left of him.'

Mary and I gave Sherlock an incredulous and irritated look, but again Thurston did nothing to disprove any of these deductions.

Suddenly, the secret agent spoke up. 'You know my motive well enough, Mary.'

Now, we turned to her; I in confusion, Sherlock with a smirk. The mask she had built up came crashing to the ground as she recognised him.

'Iggy, is that really you? I never recognised you when the car—'

'I am whoever you want me to be,' Thurston said as if he genuinely didn't care.

Mary opened and closed her mouth a few times, until I shot her a look.

'If my memory isn't wrong, it was Mr Thurston here who found out what my sister was up to. He has always been good at discovering people's secret machinations. We were at uni together, like you and Scarlett, John. I lost touch with my sister when she went to Bolivia, and after a year of not hearing from her, I assumed something was wrong. When Scarlett tried to get in touch for help, it was Iggy who picked up her trail. I can do nothing but thank you for everything you have done.'

Thurston smiled like a man who has wished for something longer than he can remember. 'I protected her because she was innocent. And it was not Eamonn who kept altering his file to put you on Scarlett's tracks. It was me. I have always loved infiltration, and the digital world is a playground for that. How would you know whom I killed, Mr Holmes?'

'You protected Mary Morstan with a vigour that was beyond usual. And you don't have the license to kill. Your hands are still shaking – you killed in a violent rage. Yet, in every other situation we've met you – and as part of your role – you are professionally calm. You would kill a man in cold blood or self-defence if that were your job. But it is not, so you single-handedly decide to kill a man for the one purpose which can supply sufficient emotion for such a deed – to protect Mary. The only opponent that required such drastic measures would be Eamonn Doyle. Am I wrong?'

Thurston smiled bitterly. It was then that I realised he loved Mary. An indescribable feeling of gaping hollowness filled me. I was jealous, but I knew I had no right to be. I had no right to anything. My eyes must have grown hollow, too, for in that moment, Mary reached out for my hand and firmly took it.

Thurston's smile grew even more bitter.

The next instant, Sherlock grabbed his coat. 'Everyone out! There's something he's not telling us. We'd better get a hold of Doyle's body before anyone else does. Mrs Hudson? Come along! And bring Mycroft, he needs to talk!'

Mrs Hudson scuttled upstairs in confusion. 'Mycroft? But he was never allowed out! How do we know it is safe out on the streets for him?'

'There's fog and he's not exactly a looker.'

And astonished as we all were, the whole party of us left the house behind and we could hear Thurston scurrying away in the opposite direction. Something told me to take my valuables with me, as the feeling of Sherlock wanting an empty house crept up on me. Mary seemed to feel the same way.

We very warily proceeded down Baker Street. It was just as we were about to turn the corner into Marylebone Street when another element of our story came full circle.

When we had met Moran, the day Scarlett – Mary – came to live with us, we'd narrowly escaped him on a river barge, only for it to blow up. Now, there was a ringing in my ears before I noticed the bang and we were pushed forward, face first, onto the ground.

For a moment, we all lay still. Another blast and another wave of pressure followed. We buried our heads under our hands, except for Sherlock who whirled around to look, his face ablaze with the reflection of flames in the fog. When another bang and a wave of pressure issued from behind us, even he had to cover his face. He turned to me. There was a mixture of confidence and anger in his eyes that stimulated my curiosity for only a moment. Then it dawned on me.

221B was on fire.

No, it can't be!

I stumbled to my feet, coughing and staggering, until I had finally picked up speed and ran towards the burning house.

What are the odds!? Why should it be 221B?

It was 221B. All our records were destroyed. My diary, Sherlock's files, Scarlett's file, the magazines! The idea of Sherlock having initialised this or having deliberately let this happened flashed across my torched brain. The last story he had found...

Is it gone? Are there only ashes left to help us stop Sherlock following its path?

In the face of the flames lashing out and around the windows and the crackling walls, I felt the lack of power to save him, to tear him away from the words on the page burn inside me.

He had known this was going to happen.

He did not want us to save him.

* * *

When John turned back to us, all hopes of it being another building crashed. Yet, I could not pretend to be surprised. We had both assumed that something was going to happen, but both of us had hoped for a burglary or a few assassins coming to kill us.

Mrs Hudson was close to tears.

John was already calling 999, but Sherlock insisted we should walk away from Baker Street. He called Mike to dig up Eamonn Doyle, and Steven, who also worked at the morgue, had volunteered to help. That wasn't going to be a smooth operation, but we weren't going to be there, so I indulged in my sadness over our home having burnt down.

As Salvatore's was an already known hideout of Sherlock's, he resolved not to go there (it now probably being somewhere else in Victorian times). Instead, he led us to the most secret of his hideouts – so secret he would not tell us where it was. At the British Museum, we took a carriage, which I noticed was heading towards the Thames.

When the door shut and Sherlock asked the cabbie not to take any more passengers, John finally let off steam. Clearly, he had thought about something I had not cared to work out yet.

'*Who* did this? You clearly know what happened,' John accused Sherlock. As the latter did not answer immediately, probably trying to rule out a few of Moriarty's assassins, John added, 'Let me rephrase. Was that magazine in there, Sherlock?'

'Yes,' the detective stammered, 'it must... Oh, no, you don't. It wasn't me.'

John was sceptical about that.

'If I had wanted to blow up my home, however Victorian, I would have left Mycroft in it.'

Mycroft just raised an eyebrow. So did John.

'Bad excuse?' Sherlock curled the bridge of his nose.

John nodded.

'Very poor reasoning indeed, Sherlock. You knew what was going to happen, yet you chose to chase me out of the house. Really, you are getting slow,' Mycroft reprimanded his little brother, then addressed John, 'He did want to destroy evidence, clearly, if you'd like to believe *my* deductive reasoning. When he called me up, I could easily spot the fuses sticking out of the books in the living room shelves. Not knowing what the instruction she had received earlier meant, Mrs Hudson called down the two homeless kids while you were gone, and gave them food. It must have been around that time that the fuses were installed.'

'What instructions!? Are you suggesting Mrs Hudson did it?' John blustered.

'I was trying to help!' the old lady defended herself. 'I received an anonymous letter earlier, it is how I have been receiving instructions until now. But this time it just said I should mind my own business and stop meddling as I was rid of my job. Jim must have finally noticed that I changed the messages slightly sometimes to help you. I only took Sadie and Finch downstairs to protect them from anyone coming in until you were back.'

'And while you were making them dinner and biscuits, Mrs Hudson, did you put out the fireplace?' Mycroft asked sharply.

'The what— Oh, no!'

We all groaned as we realised.

I wondered if she had accidentally been making her 'herbal biscuits' again.

'Just when you thought they were everywhere in Victorian times…' Mrs Hudson mumbled, very sadly.

Sherlock gave her an understanding glance.

John pouted.

* * *

It took me a while until I noticed we were heading toward Parliament Square. Under different circumstances, I might have been interested in how the famous site looked over a century ago, but as it was, my thoughts were elsewhere.

So, they had used Mrs Hudson's forgetful ways with baking, combined with the Victorian fireplace as a match, for some conveniently installed fuses in our flat. There was no way Sherlock could have overlooked this. He had probably smelled the fire before we had even left. I had to talk to Mary. The man was headed straight for his destruction, and no matter what we were to each other now, I needed her help to save him.

There was something very strange in all this. Something about his pale, worn face told me that his nerves were at their highest tension.

Suddenly, a sense of inescapability overcame me. My thoughts seemed to be rigid, like printed sentences. I recognised the voice. It didn't feel quite the same as the trance in the darkness, but it was definitely the same. An inkling of a shadow would not leave me until that fateful day we were heading towards. I should have told the others what I was hearing, but I felt that speaking the thought would give it life.

We got off at the foot of the Elizabeth Tower. Of course, Sherlock knew an 'unofficial' way in. Despite everything that had happened, a trace of a thrill passed through us all as we walked up those steps to the very top. And behind the clock face, Sherlock motioned us to sit down.

'Really? Behind the clock face of Big Ben?' Mary asked sarcastically.

'Yes, really,' Sherlock shot back. 'I once helped out the painter who did the inside of this clock room when he was falsely accused of stealing a golden watch. Fortunately, I could prove his innocence without revealing that Billy was guilty.'

'That was my best watch, you absolute prat!' Mycroft exclaimed angrily.

'I keep forgetting you're in the room... You keep your fingers off the boy, he needs the money to eat.'

Among the general patter, I finally resolved to ask about the magazine.

'Can I have a word, Sherlock?'

'No, I will not tell you what was in it,' he said, anticipating me. 'We will hide here until tomorrow morning and then I will take Mary to identify Eamonn Doyle. That is the plan and nothing else will be done without my permission. Consider yourself under constant peril of death. Nobody leaves this tower unless I say so.'

It was very hard not to hear any strange noises as the night progressed. Again and again, my thoughts felt as if they were being tempered with. I heard my voice loud and clear in my head, putting into words things that I had long had in my brain as a bitter afterthought, but none of which I had ever given any serious attention to.

𝔍𝔣 𝔥𝔢 𝔡𝔬𝔢𝔰𝔫'𝔱 𝔴𝔞𝔫𝔱 𝔶𝔬𝔲𝔯 𝔥𝔢𝔩𝔭, 𝔥𝔢 𝔡𝔢𝔰𝔢𝔯𝔳𝔢𝔰 𝔱𝔬 𝔯𝔢𝔞𝔭 𝔱𝔥𝔢 𝔯𝔢𝔴𝔞𝔯𝔡𝔰 𝔬𝔣 𝔦𝔱. 𝔥𝔢 𝔡𝔢𝔰𝔢𝔯𝔳𝔢𝔰 𝔫𝔬 𝔟𝔢𝔱𝔱𝔢𝔯.
𝔥𝔢 𝔦𝔰 𝔫𝔬𝔱 𝔴𝔬𝔯𝔱𝔥 𝔡𝔢𝔰𝔱𝔯𝔬𝔶𝔦𝔫𝔤 𝔶𝔬𝔲𝔯 𝔩𝔦𝔣𝔢 𝔣𝔬𝔯.
𝔏𝔢𝔱 𝔥𝔦𝔪 𝔤𝔢𝔱 𝔯𝔦𝔡 𝔬𝔣 𝔐𝔬𝔯𝔦𝔞𝔯𝔱𝔶, 𝔞𝔫𝔡 𝔶𝔬𝔲 𝔴𝔦𝔩𝔩 𝔟𝔢 𝔰𝔞𝔣𝔢.
𝔥𝔢 𝔨𝔫𝔬𝔴𝔰 𝔴𝔥𝔞𝔱 𝔥𝔢 𝔦𝔰 𝔡𝔬𝔦𝔫𝔤, 𝔞𝔫𝔡 𝔦𝔣 𝔥𝔢 𝔴𝔞𝔫𝔱𝔰 𝔱𝔬 𝔧𝔲𝔪𝔭, 𝔩𝔢𝔱 𝔥𝔦𝔪.

The next morning arrived far too late. Our aching limbs gave us a hard time when we tried to move.

As I slowly became fully awake, I was stung by my glaring memories of the strange thoughts I had had during the night. When I looked at Sherlock, I could see premonitions in his eyes, but only if he didn't notice me looking. The more I thought about it, and the more I remembered, I got the feeling I had a rather accurate idea of what was going to happen, as if I was about to write it down. Luckily, there wasn't a pen or paper in sight, let alone any more modern inventions.

I meant to tell Mary what I knew, hoping she'd get through to him, I meant to do so many things to prevent what was inevitably rolling towards us like a thunderstorm...

126

But Sherlock, as always, was a step ahead.

He cleverly intruded on every occasion I had deemed safe to merely ask her to speak in private. He knew me too well. I don't know if he was protecting her from it, protecting me from interfering or just determined to gamble with fate. But we both knew he was going to lose.

Some moments, I could see a faint glint of hope or confidence in the corner of his eye, but I was not convinced. Mary seemed to become more worried as she perceived the growing tension in his nerves, but she did not make an attempt to alter his plans. I hoped to God that she had figured out a plan to stop him by herself, but I didn't know how much she could see.

Does she know he has given in? Could she do anything about it? Could I? Could anyone?

How selfish of him to give in, I thought. *Why can he not stop playing the hero for us?*

It was obvious it would take a hero to stop a hero. Could I magically transform myself into one? I was tempted to listen to the voice in my head saying I should be the 𝔭𝔯𝔬𝔱𝔞𝔤𝔬𝔫𝔦𝔰𝔱 𝔬𝔣 𝔪𝔶 𝔬𝔴𝔫 𝔩𝔦𝔣𝔢 𝔣𝔦𝔫𝔞𝔩𝔩𝔶, but I knew that voice was not trying to help me save Sherlock. It had already made me kill, but I could feel it was at the very bottom of this mystery. If I found out the source, I could stop time and take control of events, stop this predetermination.

So, when Sherlock and Mary had left to identify Eamonn Doyle, I followed my ears.

Chapter 3

'Sherlock, I can't watch you do this. I don't know what it is you're facing, but can I please, just this once in your life, ask you to turn the other way?' I pleaded as we stood in the entrance hall of St Bart's, waiting for Mike to arrive.

'The game is entering its final stage. Moriarty will do anything to win. He will show his hand and be more reckless than ever before. This is my one chance at getting at him, and I cannot let it slip through my fingers,' Sherlock replied, vigour coursing through his veins.

'Please.'

Sherlock's features softened almost unnoticeably. The corner of his mouth twitched. For a long time, everything around us stopped moving. The hansom outside halted, the pitter patter of the rain subsided, the cackling seagull shut its beak. For the first time in ages it seemed, Sherlock looked at the person I really was. For the first time in ages, he looked straight into my eyes.

'You don't know what you're asking,' he said, his voice plunging into its deep satin range.

'You don't know what you're taking,' I replied.

Suddenly something in the air about him changed. His eyebrows twitched into a frown, then hardened in determination.

His lips were suddenly so close to mine, I could not have moved without kissing him. For a moment, I lost myself. I could not – would not – distinguish what was real.

When I opened my eyes, Sherlock was locked in exactly the same position as before, his lips less than an inch away from mine.

'I know.'

'There's another reason you're doing this.' I could see something stronger hidden behind his calmness. 'It's not just a game.'

Sherlock smiled ever so slightly, his eyes growing weary. 'Yes,' he admitted, but that was all he would say. Then he went through the double doors.

A few minutes later, Mike arrived and unlocked the morgue for us. When Sherlock had made sure that all the doors and windows were securely bolted, the fear of guns and intruders constantly in the air, Mike proceeded to put the corpse on the slab.

'I'm afraid Steven lost all the man's papers – I should not have given them to him – but at least I made sure to lock the door this time. So, he's in his mid-thirties, shot with a small calibre gun from a close range. Does that correspond with your agent's tale?'

Sherlock and I nodded.

'Don't worry about his papers,' he reassured her. 'They were all fake anyway.'

'Good, then brace yourselves,' Mike announced. 'He has not been stored in a cool, dry place.'

The sight was indeed gruesome. Now that I recognised the face, my emotions threatened to overwhelm me, but I felt no vision or panic attack coming over me. There they were, those dark, beady eyes, staring at me in shock, a ghostly grin on them. When I imagined his moment of death, it was as if his pale skin, though smeared with earth and mud mirrored Ignatius to me. We had always been the best of friends. I was moved by what he had done to protect me. I could see he had not just murdered Eamonn – the smile on his face spoke of supremacy in the very moment he died. I would not be surprised if he...

'...made him pull the trigger!' Sherlock concluded my thought.

'It was manslaughter surely.'

'No,' Sherlock exclaimed. 'It was all part of his plan! Suicide! He wanted to be killed and used Thurston to execute it. Oh, this is clever!'

He had found the tiny pistol he had deduced to be in Iggy's possession in the pocket of Eamonn's dinner jacket. Strangely enough, I just realised that he was dressed in Victorian clothes while Iggy was not... I did not give this any further thought though.

When Sherlock examined the weapon, he found two sets of fingerprints – one belonging to Ignatius, the other was half covered by the prints Ignatius had left, suggesting a hand over his. Of course, they corresponded with the body lying before us.

'Thurston had his gun aimed at him, but he didn't shoot. Now for some reason, Eamonn Doyle needs to be dead for his plan to work out, further suggesting henchmen to execute it. So, he takes the opportunity to provoke Thurston to the utmost, probably daring him to put his gun to his chest, and shoot him. Considering Thurston's shock after the events, I would say Eamonn likely surprised him by pulling the trigger for him.' Here Sherlock turned to me. 'Would you say that description matches his character?'

I looked down at Eamonn's frozen face and could only nod.

It was strange how his smile still tingled excitement in me, how his eyes still magnetised mine, and my horrible memories still had an unforgiving grip on me. My unbearable feeling of guilt, and the memories of my sister, did not allow me to move for a long time, but when I did, something snapped in me. It felt like I had my free will back.

When Mike and I looked at Sherlock examining Eamonn more and more closely though, we could see that *his* free will was gradually swept away.

it. There was a calling in his face, and he was going to follow it.

* * *

The voice in my head knew. It knew I was walking outright and without delay towards it. I had an instinctive feeling I was being watched and, as I should find out later, correctly so, that someone would follow me or convey the trace of my footsteps to them. First, I moved very carefully along the river to the East End, hoping for a clue to lead me into my chosen trap. I did not know that I was unknowingly following the story. I did not know that the solution would not come from the voice, but that it was drawing me in.

I should have known.

The river did not yield any clues, except that the water seemed more rapid and menacing to me, but I could not grasp it fully. Eventually, I decided to go back to Baker Street as clearly someone had known our location.

As I was walking north through Soho, I suddenly heard another voice in my head:

'𝕿𝖍𝖊𝖞 𝖘𝖊𝖙 𝖋𝖎𝖗𝖊 𝖙𝖔 𝖔𝖚𝖗 𝖗𝖔𝖔𝖒𝖘 𝖑𝖆𝖘𝖙 𝖓𝖎𝖌𝖍𝖙. 𝕹𝖔 𝖌𝖗𝖊𝖆𝖙 𝖍𝖆𝖗𝖒 𝖜𝖆𝖘 𝖉𝖔𝖓𝖊.'

It was Sherlock's voice, clear, glass-cut, but with the echoing feeling of a tempered memory. At the same time, it felt as if the words were set in stone – or rather typeset?

'𝕲𝖔𝖔𝖉 𝖍𝖊𝖆𝖛𝖊𝖓𝖘, 𝕳𝖔𝖑𝖒𝖊𝖘! 𝕿𝖍𝖎𝖘 𝖎𝖘 𝖎𝖓𝖙𝖔𝖑𝖊𝖗𝖆𝖇𝖑𝖊.' There was my voice. Invariably remembered in this ceasing sound.

As a hansom cab passed me, I again heard his voice: '𝕯𝖎𝖉 𝖞𝖔𝖚 𝖗𝖊𝖈𝖔𝖌𝖓𝖎𝖘𝖊 𝖞𝖔𝖚𝖗 𝖈𝖔𝖆𝖈𝖍𝖒𝖆𝖓?'

'𝕹𝖔,' I heard myself say.

'It was my brother Mycroft.'

131

I had not paid much attention after seeing our home burst out in flames, but I now could not remember Mycroft sitting in the carriage with us. Sooner than I realised, I accepted these facts put into my head as reality, putting aside the thought that they were forming our story before it happened rather than myself reporting what happened to us.

When I crossed Oxford Street, fog started to emerge rapidly around me. The grim, cloudy day became grimmer. It had not occurred to me in the moment that this could have been on cue, that I was setting off events by my mere footsteps. Now, I didn't know what to believe. An actor could not have been less surprised. But I walked straight ahead into Wells Street, and followed it, as if dazed by the fog, unaware of the houses that had been replaced.

The echo of Sherlock's voice in my head had shaken up my thoughts. I hadn't heard him before.

At the end of Wells Street, I vaguely made out a street sign, drawn in by the familiarity of its shape.

MORTIMER STREET, W

It seemed to me like I had lived here, for a few years at least. When, I could not remember. Suddenly, an unnatural curiosity overcame me to find my old lodgings. It did not take long. Apparently, I had had a private practice there, and a short queue of patients protruded into the street.

'Excuse me, can I help you?' I asked one of the ladies waiting outside.

'Oh, thank God, the Doctor is back! We have just been told you were out, you see. Nobody could tell us when you would return.'

It was so strange: the image of patients waiting for your return when you never knew you went out on them a century ago. I shuddered at the thought.

'Are you not well, Doctor?' the woman enquired, her sharp accent giving a threatening air to the enormous feather on her hat.

For a moment, I was frozen on the spot, when suddenly I saw a Swiss lad come running along it with a letter in his hand.

'I have been following you since the Embankment, sir!' he cried, waving the paper in urgent excitement. I took it from him and read it.

It appeared that within a very few minutes of our leaving, an English lady had arrived who was in the last stages of consumption. It was thought that she could hardly live a few hours, but it would be a great consolation to her to see an English doctor, and, if I would only return, etc. since the lady absolutely refused to see a Swiss physician...

So, I excused myself and hurried inside. Why, a Swiss lad and Swiss physicians had appeared in my thoughts I could not fathom, but I took it as overworking of my brain.

As I spoke to the first person I encountered inside, a burly man of about fifty, I could vaguely hear myself say, 'Well, I trust that she is no worse?'

A look of surprise passed over his face, and at the first quiver of his eyebrows my heart turned to lead in my breast.

'You did not write this?' I inexplicably addressed the man, pulling the letter from my pocket. 'There is no sick Englishwoman?'

'Certainly not!' he cried. 'Ha, it must have been written by that tall Englishman who came in after you had gone. He said—'

But I waited for none of the landlord's explanations.

133

I burst outside into the street again, only to find myself in the village of Meiringen in Switzerland, which I had just hurried through to treat the lady.

Now, I clearly remembered my last look in Holmes's direction.

It was impossible from that position to see the fall, but I could see the curving path which winds over the shoulder of the hill and leads to it. Along this, a man was, I remember, walking very rapidly.

I was a fool to have left Holmes! And he was a fool not to have stopped me! But then, as always, he had probably planned it this way. I could only hope I would reach Moriarty in time to stop him.

I remembered again.

I could see his black figure clearly outlined against the green behind him. I noted him, and the energy with which he walked, but he passed from my mind again as I hurried upon my errand.

Was this really Moriarty?

I had no time to think, I had to catch up and find out. Holmes had been at the top of the waterfalls, staring down at the steaming cauldron. I could still feel the cold spindrift on my face. So, I had been up there with Holmes...

Every step I took up the mountain felt like I was walking on a tightrope.

Suddenly, I was sure I had been in this village, Meiringen, all along, on a forced holiday, flying from London because Moriarty had broken out of prison. I knew my perception could not be trusted, but I had decided to follow the voice, and up that winding path, I knew, lay the solution of the mystery. Up that winding path...

Time, give me time.

* * *

Sherlock's eyes grew hollow. He had discovered something so inexplicable, he could not utter a syllable. After a few microscopic examinations, he now carefully walked over to the corpse and stared at it like an X-ray.

With two expert movements, he gripped the sides of Eamonn's face and pulled it off.

I started back as if he had initiated an earthquake. Beneath the wax was a much older man with a long scar in his face. To my utter surprise, it still looked like Eamonn, only 20 years older. His skin was all crinkled, red and tattered, and it was immediately visible that he had been wearing this mask every day for years. Only his eyes remained as young as I knew them.

'Steven said he checked him out!' Mike exclaimed defensively, and I gave her a consoling pat on the shoulder.

'This man was in the army when he was young. Quite distinguished, I'd say. Sword wound suggests fighting abroad, so he must have risen to about the rank of a colonel—'

Here Sherlock stopped dead in his tracks. '

Forget what I just said. I just need to disprove it,' he mumbled then, and we all could feel the vibration of his shaking nerves.

'Sherlock, what if you can't disprove it?'

He did not answer. What he had said was completely right, however. I could see that the scar on Eamonn's face was much broader than from a cut of a British blade, and a hook-shaped tearing at the lower end of it suggested a scimitar. Now, from the colour and state of the skin around the scar, it was clear it had been inflicted at a rather young age, but it had clearly not changed through growth, so in his twenties. The fact that he had been a soldier was less clear to me, but I could see how Sherlock had deduced his rank. There were two nasty needle wounds on his shoulder at the exact position where the flap carrying his rank would have been. Naturally, the decoration displaying the rank would have been sewn on beforehand, but it seemed like an inexperienced or incapacitated attempt had been made at reattaching them after battle, suggesting a shortage in supplies. The distance between the two stitches was covered by a square-shaped scratch. I presumed Sherlock knew this to be unique to the rank of colonel.

Returning to the present, I saw Sherlock pacing up and down the room, his mind visibly swirling around in a frantic search for an explanation. For some reason, the rank of colonel had put a theory into his head that he could not cope with. I simply could not make the connection.

While I was tracing his thoughts, I felt for a moment that the silence was artificial.

As if on cue, Steven came bursting into the morgue. He was shaking from head to toe.

'Someone just assaulted me! They threatened me with a gun, and said if I don't give you this letter in the next thirty seconds, I'll be a dead man.'

Only then did it occur to me that he was still in flimsy modern clothes, and so was Mike. Sherlock took the letter, looked at it under a desk lamp and tore it open. His face hardened in anger.

'You can't be serious!'

I quickly walked over to examine the letter.

'Next time, Steven, write better. This is a joke,' Sherlock bluffed at the pathologist.

The writing was indeed barely legible and hardly correct spelling, but I could not see what made Sherlock think that the man had written this himself.

Today is the 4th May 1891. Prove me wrong.

136

'Sherlock, what does this mean?'

'No time, no time!' he panted breathlessly, as if his throat was being strangled. 'No time!'

This was the day. The day the story was set. And this was his cue.

Sherlock stared at Steven with the rage of a storm. If first, I had expected Steven to be the victim of one of Moriarty's henchmen, that opinion had now had the tables turned on itself.

A smug grin suddenly appeared on his rat-like face.

'Sherlock Holmes in my clutches,' he murmured in a quiet, menacing way. 'You didn't see this coming, did you?'

Sherlock bitterly clenched his teeth. 'Poor attempt, Steven. I know you don't work for him. Moriarty doesn't work with idiots.'

Now Steven looked offended, but I could see Sherlock was correct.

'I'm not an idiot. I am doing a good job leading his men to you, and sooner or later he will appreciate my help.'

'Steven, you absolute prick!' Mike screamed, grabbing the feeble man by the collar and pushing him into the wall.

I would have tried to separate them, but that instant, someone shouted in through the window:

'Cab for Sherlock 'Olmes!'

Sherlock froze in his tracks. An echo of these words seemed to flicker across his face. He had heard these words before, I was sure of it. And, as if he knew that his story was sweeping him on, he slowly turned out of the room as if in a trance. I could only follow.

The detective quietly got into the hansom cab, and so did I. When we had shut the door behind us, the cabbie very hurriedly hobbled round to close the curtains. Sherlock seemed to take no notice. Of course, the cabbie could not fool him as to the route he was taking us, but did Sherlock know it already? I did not dare ask in case he was trying to hide it. I only noticed we were heading south for about three minutes, then west.

After about five minutes, Sherlock loudly knocked against the roof of the carriage to alert the cabbie to stop. Despite my expectations that we were being voluntarily abducted, we came to a whinnying halt, and Sherlock calmly stepped out of the carriage. As I did the same, I was more than impressed with the majestic sight of the blooming Strand, blackened by smog, yet untouched by both World Wars that were yet to come. This street was a pulsating vein in a powerful city, densely populated by many shops, stalls and people, much more heated in atmosphere than the empty, car-crammed equivalent which would run along the edge of the West End a hundred years later.

With a firm step, Sherlock approached a newspaper vendor.

'Fatal riot in France! Fatal riot in France! News by Special Morning Express!' the vendor was shouting into the street at the top of his voice.

Sherlock flipped him a coin and took a copy as the man raised his hat.

'Thank you very much, sir! Fatal riot in France!'

The more the man clamoured the harder it became for me to breathe. I couldn't tell if the dark fog around us affected him the same way, but black clouds coming from the harbour and Charing Cross Station gave me quite a cough. My eyes started to water, so I blinked and took the newspaper away from Sherlock to be able to read the headline.

SECOND   EDITION
SPECIAL
MORNING   EXPRESS
(BY PRIVATE WIRE)
THE LABOUR MOVEMENT.
THE FATAL RIOT IN FRANCE.
Before Friday (says the Paris correspondent of
the Standard) the name of the little town of Four-
mes was unknown to the general public...

As I tried to read on, the page started fluttering in my hand and I had to straighten it out. In doing so, I clumsily cut my finger on the edge of the paper, and an ominous drop of blood fell on the text, highlighting what I had simply overlooked.

'4th May, 1891.'

Panic rose in me. When I looked up, Sherlock had vanished in the crowd.

'Sherlock!' I cried. People started looking at me in a strange way, so I adjusted my address, 'Mr Holmes! Mr Holmes!'

At this, a man in a tattered brown jacket pointed further down the street. 'He went that way, young lady!'

'Thank you kindly, sir!' I replied, squeezing my way into the direction he had indicated. My sight wasn't the best. I had started coughing more and more, as well, but eventually, I located the emblematic deerstalker above the other hats.

As I kept pondering what on Earth had happened on this day, the date began to jump out at me fearfully from every possible corner. Pocket watches, taken out for a quick glance, glanced at me too; clocks in shop windows ticked at me mercilessly; newspapers thrust in my face continually screamed the numbers at me.

'Holmes!' I grabbed him when I reached him. 'Talk to me!'
He was staring at yet another newspaper with an empty
gaze. I shook him by the shoulders.
'What happens today!? Holmes!'
But he did not utter a single sound. Then I realised. It was
true. We were stuck in May 1891, and he could not disprove it.
He had probably examined everything he could, deduced its
authenticity and finally given up. There was no escape for him.
I started shaking him again.
'Holmes! Whatever you're seeing, it must be a trick! The
letters are wrong! Or the numbers are! Mistyped, misprinted,
anything! But it's all a big staging, do you understand!?' I cried,
begging him to come back to his senses. It took a moment until
my words reached him through the veil that was evidently
covering it. When they did, however, his eyes lit up.
'Telegraph, I must send a telegraph!'
And gone he was again.

Chapter 4

In a tingle of fear, I was already running down the village street, and making for the path which I had so lately descended. It had taken hours to come down. For all my efforts two more would pass before I would find myself at the fall of Reichenbach once more.

As I hastened up the mountain, I kept glancing down into that dreadful cauldron of swirling water and seething foam, and a feeling of draining powerlessness threatened to overtake my body every time. The path was very steep and muddy, curved by the whims of the rocks and cliffs around me. Every now and again, small bushes protruded from the stone, barring the way on the ground and above me.

My legs soon grew tired. I was out of breath before I could feel the spray around me. Still, I firmly kept on walking up and up and up. Once or twice, I slipped, and if I had questioned my ever having been up there with Holmes in the first place, I was in these moments forced to look down on the ground and could clearly see my fresh boot prints going down the hill, and even more recent, identical ones from my current steps joining them. There was no question: I had been *here* just before, not in London.

I must have imagined London, wished myself to be back at my old practice, because my brain could not bear the tragedy approaching.

I had been up by the side of the Reichenbach Fall with my friend Sherlock Holmes. A Swiss lad had called me to assist an ill Englishwoman, and I, foolishly, had followed him. The boy was nowhere to be seen now, and I had not a moment to lose, so I did not try to search for him or the man I had seen walking up. After crossing the falls on a small footbridge, the rapid water nearly unsettling my balance, I walked further up into the woods in order to reach the precipices above me.

𝔍 𝔰𝔥𝔞𝔩𝔩 𝔟𝔢 𝔟𝔯𝔦𝔢𝔣, I heard the voice in my head, 𝔞𝔫𝔡 𝔶𝔢𝔱 𝔢𝔵𝔞𝔠𝔱, 𝔦𝔫 𝔱𝔥𝔢 𝔩𝔦𝔱𝔱𝔩𝔢 𝔴𝔥𝔦𝔠𝔥 𝔯𝔢𝔪𝔞𝔦𝔫𝔰 𝔣𝔬𝔯 𝔪𝔢 𝔱𝔬 𝔱𝔢𝔩𝔩. Over and over, I could hear these words, so loudly I thought they echoed from the rocks around me.

I was becoming more and more dazed with fatigue, but I did not stop. In my haste, I overlooked a brown, wooden walking stick lying on the muddy brown ground. I stumbled over it, as I must, and fell on my knees. Cursing the owner of the stick as I scrambled back to my feet, I finally realised that this was the first sign of any human presence besides my own.

𝔍 𝔰𝔥𝔞𝔩𝔩 𝔟𝔢 𝔟𝔯𝔦𝔢𝔣, 𝔞𝔫𝔡 𝔶𝔢𝔱 𝔢𝔵𝔞𝔠𝔱, 𝔦𝔫 𝔱𝔥𝔢 𝔩𝔦𝔱𝔱𝔩𝔢 𝔴𝔥𝔦𝔠𝔥 𝔯𝔢𝔪𝔞𝔦𝔫𝔰 𝔣𝔬𝔯 𝔪𝔢 𝔱𝔬 𝔱𝔢𝔩𝔩.

I tried to shake the voice off, but in vain.

𝔍𝔱 𝔥𝔞𝔡 𝔤𝔯𝔬𝔴𝔫 𝔩𝔬𝔲𝔡𝔢𝔯 𝔰𝔱𝔦𝔩𝔩. 𝔍𝔱 𝔦𝔰 𝔫𝔬𝔱 𝔞 𝔰𝔲𝔟𝔧𝔢𝔠𝔱 𝔬𝔫 𝔴𝔥𝔦𝔠𝔥 𝔍 𝔴𝔬𝔲𝔩𝔡 𝔴𝔦𝔩𝔩𝔦𝔫𝔤𝔩𝔶 𝔡𝔴𝔢𝔩𝔩, 𝔞𝔫𝔡 𝔶𝔢𝔱 𝔍 𝔞𝔪 𝔠𝔬𝔫𝔰𝔠𝔦𝔬𝔲𝔰 𝔱𝔥𝔞𝔱 𝔞 𝔡𝔲𝔱𝔶 𝔡𝔢𝔳𝔬𝔩𝔳𝔢𝔰 𝔲𝔭𝔬𝔫 𝔪𝔢 𝔱𝔬 𝔬𝔪𝔦𝔱 𝔫𝔬 𝔡𝔢𝔱𝔞𝔦𝔩.

Holmes, of course, would immediately have deduced whom I had just been cursing, but Holmes wasn't here. Instead, I was left with the uncomfortable feeling of knowing the man who made me stumble intimately without being able to recognise or name him. I had a strong feeling it was connected to the voice in my head. It never left me and urged me now more than ever.

𝔍 𝔰𝔥𝔞𝔩𝔩 𝔟𝔢 𝔟𝔯𝔦𝔢𝔣...

I took the stick and decided to ask the owner himself. There was a second set of footprints leading further into the woods, in a direction that would lead me to the other side of the massive gorge that surrounded the falls. As I kept following the footsteps, I noticed they were exactly as wide as mine. As dazed and tired as I was feeling, I was driven by the certainty that I was heading closer to the voice in my head. It had rung out to me through the fearful ravine below me, and now it was growing louder and quieter at the same time. At first, I thought I was following a mere echo after all, but then it occurred to me.

I was approaching it from behind.

The man did not notice me approaching. His dark figure stood out menacingly in front of the lit-up leaves of the trees. For a moment, I wasn't sure if he was merely cut out, but as I came closer, I could see the tip of his ridiculous moustache. It was the man I had seen in the British Library. He had not lost his ghostly presence. I could hardly believe he had left footprints at all.

When he turned around, I nearly fell down the slope next to me.

'𝔚𝔞𝔱𝔰𝔬𝔫, 𝔍 𝔥𝔞𝔳𝔢 𝔡𝔢𝔠𝔦𝔡𝔢𝔡 𝔭𝔬𝔲 𝔴𝔦𝔩𝔩 𝔟𝔢 𝔩𝔞𝔱𝔢.'

The voice had left my head.

* * *

Back in the carriage, I tried in vain to ask Holmes what it all meant. The date, the location, his insane decision to go along with this spectacle…

His lips were sealed, not entirely voluntarily I felt.

We were now on our way to the intended destination – intended by whom I did not know. Worst of all was my sense that this destination had 'final' attached to it. If Holmes knew he had the upper hand in this, he would have given me a hint, I was certain.

At the same time, he did not look like he had resolved to lose this game. He was staring intently at the floor of the carriage, his eyes so focussed and his lips twitching, that I almost hoped he was figuring out a plan. I could not be sure.

The ride was incredibly long, and when I wanted to know where we were going, Holmes only quickly remarked, 'Iver Heath' and started looking out of the window which had its curtains closed.

'For once, I don't understand you at all,' I decided not to leave him alone. 'Usually, you are among the most predictable of people,' – here he briefly glanced up, frowning slightly – 'but now you seem to have just danced into the fog.'

'You know perfectly well how I think this is going to end,' he replied slowly, carefully, as if treading on a bog. 'And you know perfectly well I wanted that magazine burnt.'

His voice had reached its lowest pitch.

'But if you know I figured all that out, if you know Watson did, then why not tell us more?'

'I do not wish either of you to jump to the wrong conclusions,' he remarked cryptically.

I sat thinking for a long time over these three statements he had just made, and this last one turned out to be the truest of them all. It took me time to figure out what he meant, and the fact that he had said only things that were already obvious to me indicated that it was in my power, with that knowledge, to see through his plan.

So there is *a plan!*

I had only to figure it out. If Holmes had accepted that the last of his stories was upon him, he was not the kind of person to irrationally destroy evidence that would help him solve the case, no matter whether it was the first or last. He had said he wanted the magazine to be burnt, but not the story.

Either the story is not in the magazine yet or he took it with him before 221B burnt down...

But that was proof he was working on his case and hadn't dropped it yet! Warmth spread through my body and my previous lethargy began to fade. Now his first sentence held a completely different meaning.

He chose how this was going to end.

Hours later it felt, our carriage came to a halt. The coachman dismounted and opened the door. Without a word, he let us step into the open.

We found ourselves surrounded by a large park, the centre of which consisted of a large, factory-like building which was partly obscured by fog and dark clouds above us. I could not tell what time period it was from, but seeing hints of bricks at its corners, I assumed we were still in Victorian times.

I couldn't say why, but it was obvious that we were meant to enter this building, that there waiting for us was the centre of Moriarty's web, the perfect trap for Sherlock Holmes.

He stepped forward.

Instinctively, I tried to pull him back, but his steps had set something in motion that was too powerful for me to stop, and he moved ceaselessly towards the towering mass of stone. As he came close to it, water started gushing from the sky.

The stage was set.

The building in front of us was more than imposing. It had a strange air about it, as if parallel universes were converging there. It was as if thousands of stories were wound around this place, twirling about in its atmosphere, tied to the winds it exhaled... Stories, and stories about stories... tales of their creation, their transition into one world from another.

At first, I thought Holmes would dash straight into the building, but like me, the rain had riveted him to the spot. I could see his hair twisting in the story-filled air, a billowing narrative pulling at his coat. When began moving again, his steps seemed guided, but I knew he had chosen them to be.

I shook myself to follow him, but deep down, I knew there was nothing I could do. Suddenly, I knew I was not in the plot.

Why has he allowed me to come this far? There must be a way. We can't lose him, not to a story... My thoughts were going wilder than the tales around us while what was about to happen seeped through to me. I had not accepted the threat, but underestimated it.

Have I just twisted his words in my head?

In fact, I was quietly accepting his unspoken decisions, waiting for a brilliant escape plan to reveal itself or spring from his mouth.

Yes, an escape plan! That must be it! Any moment he's going to tell me, any moment...

But nothing changed. The magnetism of this place was pulling Sherlock in with a certainty that made my stomach turn.

Then, at the threshold, he stopped and turned to me. 'I think you know what I'm going to do.'

A lump formed in my throat.

After a painful moment of screaming silence, I replied quietly, 'I wish I knew how to stop you.'

'You can't stop me. I'm playing the main part,' he said with a bittersweet smile.

'But will the story follow the hero, or the hero the story? You've never escaped one yet.'

'I know, but this time, I'm not going to be the hero.'

His eyes were as poignant as his words and his intentions crystalised in my mind at last.

He was going to kill Moriarty.

'Is that how you're getting out?'

'No, it's how I'm drawing Moriarty in.'

'You think this is a good ending, don't you?' I realised in shock. 'You think killing Moriarty is all that matters?'

'If I could be assured that society was freed from Professor Moriarty, I would cheerfully bring my own career to a conclusion. I think I may go so far as to say that I have not lived wholly in vain.'

So, this was the end he was hoping for. The hope I had so terribly misjudged. He wanted to prove he had lived. To make an impact upon other lives, and save Watson's and mine from the red threads we had been entangled in.

When he saw my thoughts, he said quietly, 'Miss Morstan, will you promise me to take care of Watson?'

'Mr Holmes!'

'Will you promise me?'

I couldn't reply.

'Will you!?'

The frantic urge in his voice made me shrink. I hadn't thought of him not even planning on trying to get out. Taking in the reality of this slowly paralysed me like poison. In his desperate grip, my body dissolved and attached itself to

the stories

in the air…

billowing in the wind…

yet tied to a current

direction without mercy.

From high up, I spotted a

story I seemed to know…

I dived down with the flow of a fortunate gust of wind...

Then, I recognised it.

It was a memory of mine…

A future memory…

'Yes,' was my reply. 'Yes, I will.'

A smile of relief spread across his face which broke me yet again. I stepped in front of him, to stop him walking, and flung my arms around his neck. With all his being, he held me together, lest I burst. It was down to him that I was still in one piece …

When he let go, I was trapped inside the moment he had just cocooned me in. He had trapped me. Distantly, I seemed to hear him say, 'Remember, it is Watson who deserves you.'

But I couldn't move or react. Gently, he turned me towards the entrance of the building. The final to the destination, the problem to the case. An entrance without an exit.

I walked after Holmes only when I noticed he was gone.

On entering the building, we encountered a set of winding corridors which immediately deprived me of every sense of direction. I merely followed the seam of Holmes's coat sweeping around corners. My assigned task, I had finally understood, was to lead John out of here safely, but I was nowhere near capable. John would not be capable.

Now that it had sunk in that we would have to leave Holmes behind, I could not bring myself to face the moment. The story's climax we had all been waiting for. One point in a mere storyline – just a string of letters to those who would later read it. Our only hope was for our story to become more to its readers – a life, like it had really been to us.

Unfortunately, it was not until after the following events that I realised this.

* * *

'Do you know you are a fool not to have recognised me? I left a simple enough clue behind,' the strange man said, with a suave smile on his face.

I just shook my head angrily. 'Not everybody can be prolific. You learn that when you live with Sherlock Holmes.'

'That is precisely what I mean, my dear Watson. You see, you are me.'

'What on earth are you talking about?'

'Do you remember the book I was reading when you last saw me?'

I thought for a moment. 'The Lost World, was it?'

'You have a good memory, just like I gave you.'

'I can't follow you again.' I was becoming more enraged by the second.

'Who was the author of that book?'

It took me a while again, but when I did remember, I stood completely still. That was where I had heard the name.

'It was Arthur Conan Doyle.'

'Correct again. You see, I like you, Dr Watson. And that is why you are here. In the story, you are me.'

'Why should I listen to this?'

'You came here to ask, didn't you?'

'I came here for answers, not palaver.'

'Always to the point, the practical man through and through. I am proud you turned out so well.'

'Who are you?' I hissed at him.

'I, my dear Watson, am the man who invented you. I am your author. Call me Arthur.' He held out a hand to my petrified body. After a while, he took it back. 'I am sorry I had to put you in with Sherlock Holmes. I would much rather see you in my actual literature, not that cheap entertainment paper.'

I cocked my head. 'Your *actual* literature?'

'My historical fiction, yes. Properly researched, educationally valuable, stylistically refined. As opposed to the trivial stuff the readers of *The Strand* enjoy. You wouldn't go so far as to call these petty crime stories *literature*, would you?'

'As a matter of fact, I would not. They are our lives!'

'Oh, of course, my dear Watson. I forget how upset minor characters get when they realise they are not the protagonist. But surely, deep down, you have known a long time, haven't you?'

'It doesn't seem as if *you* like the protagonist you have chosen, *Sir.*'

'And this is precisely what brought you here. You see, I just cannot continue writing more of that trivial literature of yours. If in 100 years, I am only known as the man who invented Sherlock Holmes, then I will have considered my life a failure. Unfortunately, the public adore Holmes beyond reason, so merely not writing any more stories just won't do.'

'So, you will put an end to it that no one can expect him to come back from.'

'Exactly. One last flourish, which will hopefully earn me enough money to work comfortably until my historical fiction receives its deserved recognition.'

'We're not your characters. We exist. We lead our own lives. What makes you think you invented us? What makes you think you have any power over us? *Any* right to interfere with our life?'

'The idea of merely being a character in a book frightens people. Someone else determining the course of action can be intimidating. I understand all this, Watson, but you see, I met one Dr Joseph Bell, and I just had to write about him, however strange he was. And I was the relatable, amiable person in the whole, so I had to send *you* in there.

'But the world will soon learn that the relatable doctor has his place in the world where the perfect genius does not. Haven't you longed for this your entire life? Being the master of what happens to you, standing out and having your skills recognised? Living outside of Sherlock Holmes's shadow?'

Doyle raised a knowing eyebrow with an impish smile.

I shuddered. 'What are you going to do to him?'

'I am going to throw him off a cliff. Down the falls,' Doyle answered calmly. 'At least, I am giving him a memorable sendoff. I had the idea while spending my holidays here. Don't you think it's a wonderfully dramatic place for a showdown?'

I could not reply. Worry boiled up inside me, next to the rage. I had no reason to believe this madman, and yet...

Where is Holmes? How far away can he be? Can I still save him?

'It's a pity you can't see the cliff from here, Dr Watson. I'm sure it would make for a very heroic fall in your description. But I will see to that.' Doyle cleared his throat, and so did the cauldron below us. 'Echoes are a strange phenomenon, don't you think? Only think of the volume the splash of a human body will create. Think of the flood wave it will cause. It will make everyone turn, then the water will take it all away as if nothing had ever been there.'

I was listening to a maniac.

I had to do something.

But I could not move.

'So you're just going to have me push him, are you? The envious doctor kills the detective genius? Because that is not going to happen,' I said, my voice at its lowest.

'Oh, of course not, Doctor. I have tried to have you kill him before. It would have been quite dramatic to have the drugged best friend realise who he had shot in his delirium. But as that didn't turn out as expected, I can discard that draft. It was very handy you killed that annoying twin though. Couldn't have her in my stories – the likelihood of that! Aristotle would have been appa–'

I could not let him finish the sentence.

151

I grabbed him by the collar and slammed him into a tree, choking him until his eyes grew wide.

'Let him go, Doctor. You're not a killer. That is my job.'

I only heard the thud as I let go of Doyle. I had whirled around before I could see him hit the ground. Instead, I found myself looking at Moriarty's face. He had strangely aged decades. His reptilian face had sunk under the weight of his back, rounded by study. There could be no doubt, however, that I *was* facing James Moriarty.

I cannot remember what happened to Doyle after this.

Moriarty was the only presence in my mind. 'You!?'

'Of course, it's me! It's always me in these stories. Except I don't really appear until Holmes dies,' he said playfully. 'A bloody mistake on Doyle's part if you ask me. It's not totally ineffective, though. Nobody will ever forget me after this.'

'Do you really believe this man?'

'Of course. We are in a story, aren't we?' He let a smile dance on his slowly swaying neck. 'Let me tell you a secret. That stupid writer would never have the courage to do any of this. It's why he is running away from it. And that, in turn, is why I employed him.'

'You what!?'

Moriarty laughed a very quiet, satisfied laugh. 'You see, this is why Holmes will call me the Napoleon of Crime. Because I have committed the crime of the century!'

'The Crown Jewels, very clever.'

'Oh no, no, the Crown Jewels were merely the finishing touch...'

'There is no need for useless chatter. You clearly want to expose your genius to me, do it! It will take a lot more to impress me!'

'Well, you see, robbery – or any crime really – is simply a question of timing. If you were to go and rob a place when people

152

are there to stop you, things might get messy. I simply couldn't do that to this suit,' – he demonstratively looked himself up and down – 'so all you need to do is pick a time when there is nobody there to stop you.

'Now, wherever the Crown Jewels go, they are guarded, very carefully. That was the same in Wakefield Tower in the 19th, as in the Jewel House in the 21st century. If I wished to steal them from either of those given places at that time, I could risk committing the crime in style. If I stole the Crown Jewels from Wakefield Tower in the 21st century, however, when the guards are in Jewel House, they would realise too late what was happening, and I would succeed. You see it is quite simple. And as you know, I did succeed. I always succeed.'

'You are mad. You've completely lost your mind!' I blustered.

The shadows in Moriarty's face unsettled me, but it frightened me more to see in his eyes that he wasn't lying to me.

'You're suggesting time travel! I don't believe a word of what you're saying.'

'You're going to have to, sooner or later, Dr Watson. Because your friend will die and you will wonder how it came to that. I am by no means suggesting time travel or anything of the kind.' He mimicked a false expression of astonishment.

'Then what are you suggesting?'

'I am not suggesting anything. I have *proof* of what I have done. It is all around you.'

My eyes involuntarily moved about, but I could only see every accurate leaf and plant in its natural alpine surroundings.

What am I looking for? A crack in reality? A grain of dust in my eye? The fading edge of a hallucination?

None of them appeared.

'I take it you would like me to explain,' Moriarty carried on with unmoved gravitas. 'You have found the stories, I understand,

and you understand you are, as it were, caught inside them.' He smiled coldly. 'It is a neat little scheme, don't you think? Simple but effective. Make your enemies characters in a story. They will have to obey their writer's every whim. Control the writer and you control what happens to them.'

Gradually, it dawned on me.

'You... hired Conan Doyle... to make us into characters, so we could not escape your evil plot?'

'As always, you are a bit slow, Doctor, but then I am afraid that is your function, after all. To make Sherlock Holmes seem clever.'

I clenched my fists.

'And that,' he casually pointed his walking stick at my hands, 'is the bit of temperament he gave you, so you wouldn't be too boring a character. Still, I don't think it is enough to amuse me. Loyalty is something for dogs. In any case, to help your poor, slow mind along, all I had to do to stage the murder of Sherlock Holmes was to compel him to come to the right place at the right time. What is the one thing we are compelled to follow? The story of our own lives. Very poetic, don't you think?'

'Of course, very poetic, but time travel is where you draw the line? How did you get back into Victorian times then, if your "archenemy" was in the 21st century?'

Moriarty looked at me with pity. 'I never left, of course.'

I stumbled backwards, almost too far, trying to make sense of what he was suggesting.

'The Peelers were no match for me. They didn't even know what a fingerprint or a magnifying glass was. I needed company. A worthy enemy. In many ways, all of this is a monumental compliment.'

He looked earnest, then his eerie smile floated through the air again.

I nearly lost my balance, but Moriarty's voice kept me firmly riveted to the spot.

'If you were wondering how I transformed the world around you. I may or may not be telling the truth here, but I understand it was a simple routine of magic tricks. I cannot tell you exactly how it worked, because I wasn't there. It was my mother who did it all. She had a gift for magic that Victorian society had no value for. She had once seen Harry Houdini perform and has pursued magic ever since. Disappearing, reappearing, smoke and mirrors... Human senses can easily be confused. It was Houdini she named herself after. Hudson. Neat, don't you think? The clue was in the name all along, just like in mine.'

'You mean that Mrs Hudson turned everything Victorian around us?'

'Was there ever anybody else there who could have done it?' Moriarty grinned like the Cheshire Cat.

I could feel my head detaching from my body, floating and turning in circles.

'You see, Dr Watson, Houdini really was the key to all this. It was him who also led me to his friend, named Conan Doyle. Then a young, successless writer and physician, I found him to be my perfect prey. They are so vulnerable when they hunger for recognition. So really, it was just a question of hijacking the right post carriage at the right crossing. Suddenly, a mysterious stroke of genius gave Doyle the idea of turning his mentor Dr Bell into a detective, whose popularity would shadow Bell for the rest of his life. And thus, the shy Conan Doyle was turned into King Arthur – the ruler of your world. Of course, I immediately offered Doyle my services, should he ever need to get rid of the detective. I earned quite a profit from him, but it got boring very soon. So, I kindly suggested his putting me in exactly one of his stories to finish The Great Detective off. And this scheme of killing Sherlock Holmes a hundred years before he was ever born is, my dear

155

Doctor, the crime of the century. You see, it is not only the most *important* crime of the century, but it is the robbery of a century of time. The Boleyn pearls you found were one hundred years too young, the clothes, the furniture in your flat, my agents, everyone surrounding me was one hundred years early for your time. For months, I have pierced your 21ˢᵗ century with Victorian reality, from the moment I had my people blow up that ship with nitroglycerine bottles, slowly adding more and more Victorian antics, planting more red threads from the day Mary Morstan arrived in your lives – an obvious red thread herself, as you might have noticed – like the infrared light that destroyed Holmes's watch that day (a simple magic trick), leaving a lithium battery to be detected in a tracker (simple word play on Lily) and the red wool we hanged the beheaded doll with to remind Mary who she wasn't. There is nothing more inescapable than a classic motif, and now you are caught in my Victorian web of stories. It was really rather satisfying to see how the real world of your literary surroundings began seeping through into your brain, which held on to the 21ˢᵗ century for much longer than I expected. I concede people enjoy free will and control over their lives, but I just could not resist the temptation of burning the brain out of my archenemy. I'm sure he would not have missed out on this game for the life of him.'

'He is not going to come here,' I growled at Moriarty.

'Oh, you underestimate your friend's curiosity.'

'Whatever you've set up for him, he doesn't just walk into traps.'

'Oh no, *usually* he doesn't, but when his best friend is in danger' – his hand suddenly rushed forward as if by reflex, catching me by the throat – 'he will do anything to play my game.'

I knew we had lost when I heard Mary call my name.

Chapter 5

It was indescribable seeing John all himself again. Every emotion welled up inside me, and feeling them inside him as well was so powerful that I almost forgot myself. The fact that he was standing on top of a cliff, next to a steaming waterfall only occurred to me in a second thought. Everything here had been built artificially; it was all a fake, I was sure. It seemed the wrong way around like in a mirror, but it was designed to stage a murder. I wanted to rush over to him, but Holmes held me back.

'Don't! He only needs *one* push, and he will get it if you take one step closer,' he warned me.

'He's absolutely right, you know?' Moriarty's voice came from the shadows. 'As always, ooh, I love it when he's clever. But then, I make my little puzzles for him to solve, and you know, I'm pretty good at that, sooo… Really, he's not that clever when you think about it…'

I knew that voice… I knew it, but it couldn't be…

'Jim Moriarty, head of entertainment for tonight.'

It was so like him to announce himself.

'I always wanted a flourish, like in good old Shakespeare plays, although *he* wasn't that clever either, but since today I'm getting everything I want anyway, I'll be content with a hearty round of applause,' he declared with a slithering tongue from behind the cliff's edge.

Before I could escape my petrified state, Moriarty jumped around the rock that had been concealing him, nearly pushing John over the edge. We flinched, but with his little finger,

Moriarty pulled John back at his collar like a dog. Without letting go, he looked at me.

Jim Moriarty looked at me – Eamonn Doyle burnt my eyes out.

'Hello, darling princess,' he hissed with a sterile smile.

He wasn't Eamonn, I knew that. It was like the uncanny resemblance between Eamonn and Iggy and the dead man with Eamonn's mask on. Moriarty didn't even look like Eamonn, but his voice and manner were so similar to his that I felt as if I had just tipped myself down the waterfall. This was real. They were the same.

'Don't you see? Once you've eliminated the impossible, the impossible will eliminate you,' Moriarty sneered. 'Having your own twin is fine, but other people having siblings did not cross your mind? But then, it's not as simple as that, of course. I'm not one for disappointing solutions to a case. Eamonn Doyle, ever wondered about his name? Not that Sir Lancelot over there would bow to King Arthur if he met him. So, Eamonn Doyle, was he a brother, a friend, an acquaintance, you ask? Let me enlighten you. He was an actor. A puppet, like all of you. A lonely soldier, lost in the war, a shell waiting to be filled and turned into firework. He was my chance to make Moriarty more than a name. Moriarty is everywhere, but how does he do it? A man of a hundred faces, who lives a hundred years, but can never be caught. Eamonn wasn't the only one pulled into my web with such promises, of course. That agent you met next to the Red Circle victim – pity he forgot his lines that moment, or he would have lived. And Thurston, who saved our princess from the police. I could name more, but that would get boring. All those men are me. They say it takes murder to split a soul, and I thought, why should I keep all my genius to myself? I should be generous, and they will serve me in return. All you have to do is convince them that their empty lives and empty bodies will be remembered if you fill them with your role. Actors are vain creatures.'

He giggled, his head quavering from side to side.

'I have created an army of soldiers who all think and act the same as me. When it comes down to it, they will tell you my name in their dying breath. Every generation has their Hamlet; every generation has their Moriarty. The funniest thing is, they all think they're bringing something new to the role. Some of them are. Eamonn certainly was an exceptional example. Not so sure about Thurston. What have I done to them? Possession? Hypnosis? Drugs?' A beat. A slowly spreading smile. 'Go on, Sherlock, finish it! Tell them what I've done to them.'

Sherlock's face turned to marble. Realisation seeped through his paralysis, bitterness dripped from his voice.

'You put them on stage. Limelight works better than any drug. More effective, more addictive.'

'Correct!' Moriarty cried out. 'The addict worked it out himself. I can always rely on you to deliver on cue. Just like my mother. I wish she didn't grow to like you as much. I was almost worried she would stop you coming here, but then you can't resist me, can you?'

'And then there is Miss Morstan, my personally hired traitor in my brother's organisation, the perfect casting. Did nobody tell you when you were young, Mr Holmes, that traitors are dangerous people to trust? Look at you, *all of you*! One little calculated misinterpretation on his part, and you're standing just where I invited you when I first met you. You've got to understand the gratification he's giving me, playing my game to lose. You see, people with a moral code of any kind are so predictable. I pull one little string, and everything is his fault. And the charge? Ancient, really, nothing new. Hubris killed Icarus, and hubris will kill Sherlock Holmes. You miscalculated. Writing outweighs character.'

I couldn't believe it. All this, Holmes's fault. I didn't mind so much that I was back where I deserved to be, but that Holmes had given himself up so willingly from the very beginning…

He seemed so far away, although he was standing right next to me. His whole countenance had congealed to a solid rock around him. He was standing rigidly upright, his hands behind his back, his look tied to Moriarty's eyes like steel blades that only softened at the sound of John's voice.

'Holmes! Tell him what really happened! Prove that you know how he did it!'

A flash of light escaped Holmes's eyes. His face began to tense as his mind changed from defence to offence.

'Bluescreen,' he cried, and the echoes came down on us in showers.

Moriarty held still.

'He used a bluescreen to cover the Crown Jewels and manipulated the security cameras to filter out any blue elements they were recording. A simple device. If all his men dressed up in blue, and the filtered-out masks in the footage were covered by footage of the empty room from an undetected underlying video, they would be practically invisible on CCTV. That way they could also easily cover the jewels and shift them to Wakefield Tower while the guards were busying themselves with other things as nothing happened on the footage. The same trick again at Wakefield Tower, when everybody thinks they are prepared and position themselves in front of Jewel House. Nobody is there to stop you, and at the same time you incite the image of stealing the Crown Jewels from a different century,' Holmes explained calmly.

'What about the pearls!?' Moriarty shouted almost gruffly.

'Simple,' Holmes replied languidly. 'They are not Anne Boleyn's pearls. They belonged to a later necklace made for the Boleyn family – same design, same traces of use and position, hence the beautiful myth that links the Imperial State Crown to the revolutionary Tudor queen. But it is only a myth.'

For a moment, there was silence. Only the falls thundered down the sharp-edged rocks to both sides of it into the deep cauldron below us. Holmes and I were standing on the edge directly opposite a precipice on the other side, where Moriarty had caught John. There was no time to wonder why or how he had come here. Moriarty was thinking, calculating within split seconds. Eventually, a bitter smile appeared on his face.

'That proves nothing! A few cheap tricks will not explain the whole affair and you know it, Sherlock Holmes!'

And then he gave John a quick, strong push.

To both Holmes and my astonishment, we could now see that he had pushed him in the other direction, away from the fall.

John was lying on the ground, petrified.

'I dare you, Sherlock Holmes, to come over and fight me,' Moriarty cried savagely. 'Or your petty friend will die!'

He pulled a small gun from the pocket of his long, dark coat and aimed it at John.

'Bring the woman and they will both die,' Moriarty jeered, his eyes narrowing to reptilian slits.

I tried to hold Holmes back. I knew how this was supposed to end. There was no need to read the story; I could read it in his face.

But Sherlock Holmes would not be held back.

Instead, he called out, 'We have a gentlemen's agreement, then! I ask only for a moment of privacy!'

Moriarty pursed his lips. 'No foul tricks, Holmes. Leave those to me.'

So, quietly, Holmes turned to me, cutting off my view of John and Moriarty, and clasped my upper arms. 'Do not interfere,

Mary. Trust me. I know what I am doing. Have you ever seen me lose a fight?'

I had to shake my head.

'I will fill the cracks in the walls that he opened. Bear that in mind, Mary, and I will be back.'

He looked down into my eyes very sternly.

'Take this,' he said, his voice as low as the cauldron. Carefully shielding a battered, rolled-up piece of paper from the spray, he took my angry fist, opened it and closed my fingers around the letter. It was addressed to John.

My heart sank. Tears filled my eyes, mixed with the spray, and before I could see again, he was gone.

It was as if I had burst into a million waterdrops, following gravity among the spray. The edges of the rocks splintered me, the friction of the current evaporated me…

I could not move or John would die. A sense of the story being shaped in this very moment nailed me to the spot.

If I interfere, can I change it? What would happen then? Will we all break free or vanish from existence?

As Holmes made his way to the other side, I locked eyes with John. I had not expected what I saw in them and faltered. A pebble fell down into the chasm. He'd had an idea.

Suddenly, the fear of a fatal mistake coursed through my body like an electric current. As Holmes emerged from the woods behind Moriarty, the voltage increased. The next instant, it was past the limit.

John… had run away. *He has left him for dead!* my head cried, but my body was transfixed by the current of the story.

* * *

This was my only chance. The only chance to make a difference. I didn't know why I thought it would work, or how, but the impulse to run away was so strong, I could not resist it. If Conan Doyle was to write about Holmes's death, he would have to do it through my eyes. Over my dead body! I would not give him the opportunity.

It began to rain.

If I wasn't there to witness Sherlock's death, no one could record it. It wouldn't be the epic end of the world's greatest detective. There would be a gap in the story.

Gushes of water came from the sky. As I was running, my head grew dizzy. The ground became slippery. This was the only idea I could hold on to. If I wasn't there to see him die, no story would come of it. Instead, nothing would be predetermined by my writing, Conan Doyle's writing or anything! It would all be a mystery that nobody knew the answer to. Sherlock would be free to save himself.

Branches, twigs and leaves beat into my face as I gathered speed. The water was flooding down at me. I started tumbling. There is no story to tell. *I* would not tell the story of Sherlock Holmes's death.

* * *

I had long stopped caring about what would happen if I moved. John had run away. He was out of danger, but he had betrayed Holmes. All I wanted was not to abandon him too.

Then everything happened so quickly. I could not hope to reach him in time, but something in me could not tear my eyes away.

Moriarty was still laughing at the cowardice of Holmes's loyal companion, when the detective darted forward and tackled him. The old maths professor proved unnaturally strong, almost completely resisting Holmes's force. Yet, with a clever grip and a kick at Moriarty's side, Holmes suddenly wrenched the walking stick from his adversary. Moving daringly close to the edge, he thrust the stick at Moriarty's gun and sent it soaring into the abyss.

To my horror, Moriarty gave a short and terrifying laugh, then threw himself at Holmes with all his might. For a moment, they both threatened to tip over the edge.

A few expert grips, executed with calmness and precision on Holmes's part, weakened his opponent and he managed to push him forward against the rock.

One second long, there was a perfect power balance, the strength and strategies of both men sizzling in the air. One second long, I could see the chess board in their eyes. One second long, they calculated. Then they agreed. There was a flash in both their gazes, a unanimous movement towards each other, their dark coats billowing high. My perception slowed down. They turned around as they wrestled and then tumbled.

The gushing of the waterfall drowned my voice.

Holmes pushed—

—Moriarty pulled

and together they fell.

As Holmes's foot lost touch with the tip of the precipice, his eyes caught mine in one final gaze.

It was a smile of victory.

Then the weight of Moriarty's body pulled him down into the gaping chasm, and the water closed its mouth around them. With a scream stuck in my throat, my heart pulled me to the edge, but I could see no more. The was spray and steam everywhere. He'd really done it. He'd danced into the fog.

'*Sherlock!*'

Then a thud, a splash, tearing my ears apart. The echo of the crash reverberated up the chasm, louder and clearer with every second, mercilessly forcing itself into my brain, into my conscience. I closed my eyes and felt the vibration shaking my body. When I opened them again, there was a hand holding my upper arm. I took no notice.

I kept staring down the fall. I could still see him falling. I could still look into his eyes. My vision was shaking, reverberating.

I blinked.

There, on the rocks below— there was something strange. It was like another rock had grown out of the wall of stone. Another hand on my arm. I started writhing and struggling. Suddenly, a massive boulder thundered down from high above my head and plunged down into the cauldron. There was a loud crash, and I was pulled away from the precipice.

* * *

The water stopped abruptly. The ground under my feet started turning. From the fog emerged two dark shapes. My thoughts were swirling, my legs twitching and my heart burst with regret. When the ground had turned 180 degrees, I ran away from my pursuers back towards the fall. Adrenaline kicked in; I was faster than ever. But as I skidded to a halt on the cliff, I could see the marks of combat on the ground and blood in the savage waves below me.

Sherlock Holmes was dead. And I had left him to his demise.

I had not prevented the story; I had only abandoned my friend to die. The thunder and splashing took turns to grind my mind to pieces. I broke down on my knees under the weight. My eyes were covered. Two strong hands clutched my arms from behind. I took no notice. I let them drag me away, hoping I would wake up. Instead, I heard distant cries of

'Fire! Fire!'

Only moments later, I was pushed through a soundproof door into a corridor. Lights were flashing – I wasn't sure if I was in a hospital. There was a crowd of people all wearing the same dark clothes – did I say hospital? Lights flashed. Or flickered?

'Fire! *Fire!*

'What is it, Postance?' someone shouted.

Another stranger had come in. 'There's a fire in my study! The documents! The documents will all be destroyed! Evacuate the building!'

At the time, I attributed this to an unsettling fantasy unleashed by my trauma. But I was wrong. The red lights flashing with the word 'Live' and doors labelled 'Studio 1' and 'Studio 2' were real.

The police arrived only moments later. I was dragged into a car, and Lestrade drove me away, speeding past a sign reading PINEWOOD.

'Several streets are on fire!' he was shouting at me. 'There's black smoke everywhere. It's like the whole city is burning! How could this get so out of hand!? Everything points towards the fire having started in Baker Street! John!? Can you hear me?'

Chapter 6

My hands were cuffed to a clean white prison bed when I woke up. The smoke had taken me out. When I turned around, I noticed black dust all around me. My hair had been scorched. 'You made a narrow escape, they tell me,' John said, ambling into my cell in my frantic imagination.

I had seen him so clearly so many times that when he actually appeared, I did not believe my senses. Several days passed before they admitted him to me. Several days for my sore eyes to dig into the frayed piece of paper in the pocket on my chest. Several ages for me to understand. It was a letter to John.

My dear Watson,
John,

I write this to you in the full confidence that I will have vanquished Moriarty at the Reichenbach Falls. It is important that I explain my actions. I have found Moriarty's hiring of certain people to be at the heart of the web he has chained our lives to. I cannot yet account for everything, I must admit, but you know my methods. Once Toby has cracked my password, please open the file 'M' on my computer. You will find all the information you need in there. Keep my armchair where I like it. Trust Mrs Hudson. Trust Lestrade. And most of all, trust Mary. Give my love to her, and know me to be your true friend,

Sherlock Holmes.

* * *

Lestrade had saved both our lives. Without him, I would have never seen Mary again. The evidence against us was bad, and we were granted no more than fifteen minutes in the same cell.

When the door opened in front of me, I was at first taken aback by how distant she seemed. She was not fully awake. Her hair was covered in ash.

I reached out to her. She twitched, smiled, then grasped my hand as if I was holding her above the abyss. But when she spoke, she had lost her belief in reality.

'John, how much I wish it were you and not myself I am talking to. You know, I've been talking to you a lot lately. I miss you so much. I just wish everything were different. Can I hold your hand?'

Her voice was hoarse from speaking and crying. Only too willingly did I give my hand to her.

'If you could see through my eyes now, John, you would be surprised how well I remember your face. And that's your hand – every detail of it as I remember.' She stroked it with a melancholy smile. 'It feels so real, I feel really quite close to you sometimes.'

It took me an eternity to shake her out of her trance. Even embracing her would not do it, but when she heard the grief in my voice asking her to wake up, she flinched, then looked at me closely.

'It *is* you, isn't it?' Mary ran her fingers across my face. 'They finally had mercy on me.'

I smiled at her, my smile broken as hers, our hearts empty and yet full of everything.

'John, John, please forgive me. Please forgive me for everything I have done to you. Forgive me for being a lie.'

I only held her tighter.

'You, Mary Morstan, are the best thing that could have happened to me. I've been blind and deaf the last few weeks. Let me bury your past and give you a present.'

'If only there were a present to flee to,' she sighed, holding on to me. Then she tore herself away from me. Before I could move, she had clasped my hand and I could feel something in it. With red eyes, she stared at me and closed my fingers around the letter.

'It's from Sherlock. We must do as he says.'

I nodded.

'We mustn't forget him, John. Never, do you hear me?'

I nodded again.

'We will make the world remember him,' she insisted, and I smiled.

Two minutes before our time was over, Lestrade opened the barred window for us and let a ladder down. It was night-time and he had deliberately fixed the flashlights in the wrong position. Mrs Hudson waited downstairs in her car. She spoke only a few words at the gate.

We were free.

Back at what remained of Baker Street, she gave us Sherlock's laptop and announced she was renovating.

'Well, he wants his armchair where he likes it,' she said, her voice shaking. She quickly busied herself replacing a few burnt or broken things.

Lestrade did his best to cover our tracks, so we had a couple of days to dig into our memories of Sherlock, which were falling apart.

Mary cut her hair and I had new passports made for us, as Lily and Hamish Watson. We prepared for a new life, but as we scoured the flat for touches of Sherlock's life, we turned more and more into the burnt wreck that was around us. Nothing would

169

mend what the fire had taken. Water puts out fire, but it drowns the ashes that remain. There was no time to heal, no means of hiding from the gaping absence that had ripped a hole through our existence.

We will run, we will hide, to save his legacy and defeat Moriarty's web. We cannot rest. Unless our friend were there waiting for us in his armchair when we return.

To my amazement, I found my diary in a fireproof box in the cupboard, with a note attached to it.

In your words only, John.

I knew what I had to do. I knew I had to write. I had to tell the truth before other accounts would blacken the pages holding on to the man whom I shall ever consider the best and wisest friend I have ever known.

However far we have come in the world, we could see empty faces like ours, people with black ribbons around their arms, the whole world seemed in mourning for Sherlock Holmes. Questions were flooding in from all the world, but I did not answer them. I had to tell the whole story to answer the question that it all came down to.

Having written it all down, I can only repeat the words I have chased since the fall.

When did we lose our friends to fiction?

When did we lose our heroes to history?

170

When we lost our dreams to sleep, John…

Epilogue: Elegy's End

Where are you now, Sherlock Holmes? Where are you dancing? I know you're dancing. I can see you in my mind. Don't think you can escape me.

I will say everything out loud here, but I will have to start at the beginning.

Colonel Moriarty's vicious accounts of the murder he was certain Sherlock Holmes had committed have entirely taken over the press. John's long silence was seen as defeat after his friend killed an innocent Maths professor. But we were in hiding and it was hard to disprove a dead man's word. The secret service tempered with the colonel's corpse to ensure the files did not record one of their men killing him. Thus, the colonel's posthumous letters to the press were declared not posthumous at all, but that the colonel had apparently died a few days later. This was seen as further evidence against Sherlock Holmes.

When John wasn't looking, I've been poking my nose into his things. A week ago, he had to thank me. In the fireproof box between his diaries, I found the magazine. December issue, 1893. It struck me as odd that the cover was printed on white paper rather than the usual light blue. When I pointed it out to John, he was startled. At first, he was reluctant to open it or examine it more closely. Instead, I took it back and thumbed through it. There were unusually many typos and the layout didn't seem quite right in a few places. Then it jumped at me – there were blank pages! About twenty of them. And between them lay a tiny note:

Awaiting Watson's story urgently!

When I showed it to John, he was puzzled and angry. 'How could he do that!? How could he do this to us! It wasn't written down yet!? He had nothing to follow!? Nothing forcing him!? All his premonition a hoax!?'

'Not his premonition, I don't think, John. His premonition was there, but the suggestion that it was based on the story was deliberately false. In any case, John, someone *has to* write it. Someone has to set it right. We can't let Sherlock be remembered as a murderer.'

How often my mind wandered back out into the spray of the Reichenbach Fall. It was a compulsion so unnatural and so painful, I was beside myself for a long time. But now I know. That half of his violin which survived the fire gave me the hint. There was something hidden in my coiled-up memory again, a clue he had given me. I searched for it frantically, depriving myself of sleep for several nights like Sherlock had sometimes used to do, when it occurred to me.

'I will fill the cracks in the walls that he opened.'

He had told me to keep this in mind and he would be back. Without telling John, I started searching the house. If Sherlock had meant for John to know, he would have told him, not me. So, I decided to keep this to myself. After all I didn't know what it would lead to.

I found an envelope addressed to 'Mary' behind the wallpaper of 221C. I know Sherlock meant for me to find it.

Mary,
I am glad I could rely on your memory once more. I trust in your discretion when reading this, so overleaf you will find a name which I think is at the centre of our mystery. Your talent at deductive reasoning compels me to ask you to solve it. Please forgive any inconvenience my absence is causing

173

you. Tell John he saved me. But don't answer any questions.
Please, forgive my absence, Mary, and believe me to be
Truly yours,
S

With trembling fingers, I turned the paper around…

Mary Foley

It took me less than ten seconds to find out that she was the mother of Arthur Conan Doyle. As I start to dig deeper, I realise what Sherlock wanted me to do. She was the one who persuaded Conan Doyle, and I am going to be the one to persuade her.

I have written down everything, as best I can remember, and I remember the odd shadow that had appeared out of nowhere among the others under the waterfall, the spray in my eyes, John's absence and the stone that had fallen down, how closely it had seemed to be aimed at the new shadow and how the shadow was clinging to a lower precipice.

The pieces of the puzzle come together as I write…

I know where you are dancing. I can see you now, I can see you and your puzzle and I cannot but smile and shake my head at you.

I posted the letter in your envelope just this morning. What a strange phenomenon time is. *What a strange phenomenon you are, Sherlock Holmes. Why is it when you're dancing it is always on our noses?*

There is a knock on the door.

Excuse me, dear reader, while I answer it.

174